PROMISES

Part 3

Affairs of the Heart Series ~ London

KEW TOWNSEND

Tremmelle Publishing

HOLLYWOOD, CALIFORNIA

© 2016 Tremmelle Publishing. United States
© 2015 Cover Design by Sparkle Graphics
© 2015 Cover Layout by Jesse Kimmel-Freeman
© 2015 Cover images by Imagesolutions; By-Studio
© 2014 Book Cover and Layout by BookDesignTemplates.com

Sign up for NEWSLETTER at www.kewtownsend.com

PROMISES/ KEW Townsend
ISBN 978-06924989-8-9

Affairs of the Heart Series
London

HEART (Part 1)
TEMPTATION (Part 2)
PROMISES (Part 3)

Forthcoming

DEVOTED (Part 4)
BETRAYAL (Part 5)

Sign up for Newsletter

kewtownsend.com

CONTENTS

Chapter One

IN ANOTHER LAND

1989

Briarwood Estate, Surrey County, England

Day 3

The timeless fairy tale landscape of the English countryside held Holly Hill spellbound. It was as ethereal as she'd imagined. A perfect, lush, dew-drenched garden in Eden and incomparable to the drawings in the picture books her father read to her as a child.

Holly rode with Kaine Walker, in quiet serenity, the only sound the melodic purr of the motorbike's engine as he followed the endless winding road. Kaine was in no apparent hurry to arrive at their destination.

A single black cloud dotted the periwinkle blue sky.

She hoped it wasn't an omen.

Luka....

She would see him soon. Did Luka Hunter truly understand?

The stabbing apprehension settled in her stomach said she didn't think so.

A carload of teenage girls shrieked loudly, bursting in to disturb their peace. Kaine quickly darted down a wooded lane and hid the motorcycle behind a giant tree.

"How did you know about this?" Holly queried as she swung her leg to dismount the bike.

"Spent a lot of time here. Forget that, come closer to me, girlfriend," he demanded sweeping her into his arms. He kissed her with expectations of a marvelous love to come. They stood beneath the tree hidden from the world, stealing a few precious seconds. After a spellbinding kiss, Kaine unbraided his body from hers. He reached into his saddlebag, pulled out a mineral water, a small container of cubed cheese, and sliced French bread to share.

"Thirsty? Hungry?" he asked, smiling at her with an incredible glow.

"Don't we have to get going? Isn't Luka expecting us?" She speculated aloud, wondering why she would choose to mention Luka to Kaine. She thought back to how tense Luka's voice had been on the phone.

Get Kaine dressed straightaway. Will ya?

"Fuck Luka! This is our date. Don't we need a meal to

make it one?" Kaine argued.

A tiny smile softened the harsh edges around his lips.

"I'm sorry. It's … he can wait. I want you all to myself for as long as possible."

Kaine's words warmed her as she leaned against the rough bark of the tree. Kaine dropped to his haunches and pulled her down beside him.

She sat resting on a tuft of tall, green grass and tucked her feet under her.

Kaine twisted the trunk of his upper body and swiftly laid his head in her lap gazing starry-eyed up into hers.

A light spin of dizziness washed over her looking at him and decided to share her feelings. "You make me breathless, Kaine Walker," she praised.

He squeezed her hand and remained quiet. His Technicolor blue eyes burned with the same wonderment of her.

They sat lost in the marvel of each other. Her fingertips traced the line of his chin, and then playfully wrapped her fingers around the breeze driven locks of his soft dark hair. He occupied himself with her other hand kissing each pad of her fingertips. His lips felt warm against her cool fingers.

Holly started to speak, but he placed her fingers in his mouth. His eyes whispered to be still.

The soft sounds of the birds singing in the countryside filled the enchanting scenery. The wonder of Kaine settled in, and her words of contentment road the crest of a ragged breath. She spoke in a soft, sentimental tone.

"I've found real happiness with you."

As soon as the words had tumbled from her lips, she thought about how like Adam and Eve they were. No one but them in the world, but there would come a time when they'd have to leave the enchanted garden — to face Luka — the snake. Or, was he the apple of temptation? And if she succumbed to him what would her punishment be — banishment from the Garden, from Kaine?

She bent down to kiss her dream man Kaine as he pulled himself up a bit to lean on her chest. She cradled his head, and they lingered for long moments in the newness of each other.

Kaine's hand slid up around her neck and pulled her closer, then closer still to within an inch of his sweet breath. His lips pressed hers, warm, and soft, his tongue pushed between her lips, diving deep, kissing her until she no longer remembered where she was or cared. The soft curves of her upper body molded to his hard form as she ached for him, falling deeper and deeper into the enchanted spell with the man named Kaine.

"There he is. There's Kaine." The high-pitched, teenage voices yelled, and the squeal of tires tore into their private inner sanctum.

Kaine reluctantly broke the kiss, "Fuck!"

Holly's head reeled as Kaine jerked her to her feet and quickly pulled her to the bike. The posse of girls was too close. Seconds later, Kaine sat on the motorbike, twisting to check if she was safe aboard, and ready. She gave him a sharp nod and held on tightly. He released the brake and sped off down the secluded country road at breakneck speed, leaving a white cloud of dust in their wake. He continued down the road until it ended at a mountainous gate with old, carved piles on both sides. A black iron fence stretched lazily across both sides of the road into infinity. An archway of twisted black iron announced their arrival to *BRIARWOOD*.

Kaine abruptly stopped, quickly punched in the security code and wa ... la. The back tire of the motorbike spat out the gravel as Kaine barely made it inside to safety. The girls caught up with them and scrambled to slip to the other side of the massive electronic gate before it slammed shut. They weren't fast enough.

Kaine turned to Holly, shrugged his shoulders and admitted with a boyish grin. "They love me."

As Holly rode along she soaked up the extraordinary countryside, she was sure ever created. They drove through two separate forests, some thicket, and under a long, tree-lined canopy lane. The winding road reminded her of the opening scene of the novel *Rebecca*. This spectacular entrance was how she'd pictured the road to Manderley. Only, Briarwood was vibrant, alive, and well attended. They traveled endlessly along the serpentine paved road. She passed the most exquisitely woven color pallets of varying greens and earth tones from the flora and fauna landscaping, she'd ever seen.

Holly conferred quietly with herself. "Who can afford to live here?"

They eventually arrived at a clearing high atop another green rolling knoll. She noticed the three sides around them created a long green valley. On her right, a small mountain climbed high to touch the dark clouds. Kaine reached out and pointed. Perched on the flat summit of the mountain was a tall fortress.

An English castle.

Her first English castle and it sent a quick chill up her spine. Tall and imposing, the turrets of the walls pierced the swarm of black and gray clouds that protectively surrounded it and denied the sun. The imposing group of domineering clouds welcomed the tiny black cloud that had been trailing them as if it were the Prodigal Son arriving home.

The excitement quickly wore off and as they approached the fortress from the times of kings and queens. Holly thought the dark, gloomy castle was better suited for a spooky or haunted horror movie, then a rock video. Another cold shiver pricks her spine. This was where she was to spend the rest of her day with Kaine and Luka? Unexpectedly, apprehension froze her thoughts. She didn't want to go any further.

Her instincts said leave.

Run.

The concerns started to crystallize, back in the dark corridor of her mind, as she watched the crimson blood oozing, dripping down the side of the white basin into a slick puddle. Holly shook her head to clear it, but it was no use, her feelings of torment clung to her memories as a child's night terror.

A light gray mist rolled out to greet them, crawling along the ground as the motorcycle hummed, climbing the short, but steep, switchback road leading to the bold entrance. A cold wind kicked up, encouraging the impending storm to arrive quickly. Once more, despair flooded her, and a strong, compelling urge to turn, and run from this sinister place.

But, it was too late.

By the time, she and Kaine drove to the edge of the dark and spooky Grimm's style castle, she'd warmed slightly to the monstrous structure. Close up it wasn't as imposing. In fact, it had a particular enchantment she wouldn't have expected moments earlier. She welcomed the release of the negative feelings, before their anticipated arrival.

She scanned the hundred-and-eighty-degree view only to be visited by a momentary bite of disappointment. Where was the obligatory murky moat to surround the mammoth structure?

Kaine continued forward and the closer she approached the fortress, the more bewitched she became. When she arrived, the pictures in her imagination had her under the magical spell of thrones and ballrooms, surprised the castle was the same foreboding citadel from a distance.

The mammoth castle sat on the flat land. At the foot of the thirteenth-century stonewall, the thick gray mist danced unnaturally, playing, and turning somersaults like joy-filled children. If her history served her, this bastion would have been the rough keep of a long forgotten Warlord. Or, possibly, the seat of power. Perhaps a frequent destination for royalty. The crenelated wall, shaped into a rectangle that protected the inner sanctuary, also had round piercing towers, and square turrets standing as old centaurs at each corner, decorated with brightly colored flags, embosses with a coat of arms. They were waving in the wind, announcing their arrival, and inviting her to enter.

"Who currently lives in Briarwood Castle?" she asked aloud.

Kaine hadn't heard, and his body grew rigid. Something was wrong.

Holly's stomach pitched slightly as they passed under the thick outer wall. What were these new feelings of intrepidation? Were their anxieties taunting them because soon they would face Luka?

Holly wanted off the bike. She needed to settle her stomach and explore the extraordinary gift of Briarwood Castle. The sheer colossal size of the five-story stronghold was unexpected. It commanded her awe and respect all the while the gray mist continued to thicken.

The massive, thick, green vine, woven itself around the grand wall, in, and out of the holes blown into the outer crust of the fortress. Luxurious plush greenery, lovingly wrapped itself on the wall, like green, velvet, cloak to protect it. Various shades of green bushes and patches of pastel flowers sat respectfully at the foot of the gray, brick walls like an embroidered tapestry.

Then the wondrous arrival was pierced by the long anticipated voice. "Where the bloody hell have you two been? Nearly all the fucking morning's gone!" Luka yelled frantically as he glared at Kaine. He appeared from thin air as if by magic. His facial expression pinched with anger, and his eyes filled with a heavy dose of betrayal. Luka would not look at her.

The guilt condemned her, stabbing her in the heart.

Luka whirled on his heels stomped away muttering aloud. "I don't bloody well want to know." Then he yelled, "Lil, take Holly. Nigel takes Kaine. Get them ready straightaway. We're losing the light. It was a bloody bad idea to shoot on location instead of at the studios. This mist is rising from the damp earth like bloody restless spirits of the dead."

Luka kept walking. His brittle body language was telling Holly he was not happy at all causing the sheepish grin on her face to fade into humiliation. The dense, breeze-driven, billowing black, and gray clouds agreed with Luka and rushed in to cover what was left of the blue sky. They were menacing as if swirling with anger and pointing their fingers at her.

He'd believed he'd start again with her. But she had betrayed him. Her head hung in shame.

Kaine squeezed her hand and gave her a look of 'it will be all right.'

Holly wasn't so sure.

Kaine left with Nigel, the hairdresser.

Holly glanced up at the castle, such a powerful backdrop for Lilly's timely arrival. The thin brunette approached and flashed Holly a big, warm smile.

"Oh, Lil," Holly sighed needing a friend. "A castle, a real ivy-covered castle," she announced, charmed by the astonishing structure.

"It's another cold, damp castle, Holly. Been here for centuries and in desperate need of repair. England's bloody full of them." Lilly informed her with no interest for adventure in her voice.

That's not what Holly saw. The enchanted spell was working. Briarwood Castle, the perfect backdrop to spin romantic fantasies, scene after scene, casting Kaine as the prince, and she a princess.

What of Luka?

Luka, she lamented, as her heart sank. What part would he play? How could she have been so thoughtless to disappoint him and be so excited about being Kaine's secret girlfriend?

Assigned to separate make-up areas in the massive east wing, Peter finished with Kaine. He was waiting when Lilly took her to him.

"Hello, my pretty." Peter complimented, his eyes beaming.

"I've been looking forward to working with your magnificent hair."

Peter finished the top pulling large strands back into braids, twisted and secured them with hidden combs. The back hung in long finger curls. Peter tamed the wisps of hair near her forehead, clustering them into coiled tendrils to frame her face. Afterward, Peter painstakingly wove in Baby's Breath flowers.

Holly followed Lilly to a small, chilly room, apparently used for storage of sorts. It doubled as a private dressing area. Lilly helped Holly into a corset, once a traditional foundation undergarment, indicative of the Olde English style of dress.

Holly shivered from the cold temperature of the castle in spite of a small electric heater sitting in the corner struggling to heat the tiny space.

"I was hoping this authentic lingerie might put you in a romantic mood," Lilly explained.

Holly smiled. "This whole place puts me in a romantic mood. I no longer in the twentieth century. I'm cast into a magical whirlpool that is swallowing me whole and whisking me back to the twelfth century."

Lilly dressed Holly in the odd-looking corset with flexible, thin, steel strips covered with silk. Lilly fought with the corset.

"Blast this. Bloody hard to catch this last row of hooks," she complained as she fastened her into the contraption.

Holly tried to breathe normally. "I think I'm going to faint." She warned grappling for breath and then leaned against a piling that braced the ceiling. Her waist was the tiniest she'd ever seen it, and her breasts were crushed flat, causing her a high amount of misery. "How am I supposed to wear this for five minutes let alone hours? What a woman in any century won't do to look beautiful," she muttered under her breath.

"I'll see what I can find to make you more comfortable." Lilly consoled as she stopped at the doorway.

Holly looked up to see why Lilly stood so still. She twisted at the waist causing the steel ribs of the corset. They cut deep into her flesh, and about to cry out from the torture when she saw what blocked Lilly's departure.

Chapter Two

CARELESS WHISPERS

The stabbing pain in her flesh was nothing compared to the stabbing pain of betrayal in her heart as she looked upon Luka. He stood inside the doorway, and his beautiful sky blue eyes said it all. They burned hot. Holly grabbed for a breath that wouldn't come. The searing waves of forbidden pleasure flashed as lightning bolts spreading quickly inside her — Luka — how stunning. She'd missed him. The familiar heat raced at breakneck speed through her bloodstream. Now, what the hell was she to do? Should she stop staring at him, and cover her half-naked body, or run to him.

Too late.

Luka made the choice for her.

"Blast! Lil? I don't like this! Do I need to attend to every detail?" He stormed.

Lilly trembled from Luka's verbal explosion.

Luka's face grimaced, but then he apologized.

"Sorry, Lil, I didn't mean to go ballistic. I hate exterior

shots. Too much is left to chance. I'm up against this bloody impossible weather. Holly is due on the set straightaway, and wardrobe is all wrong. I'll have to stay and help Holly if we are to get things moving straightaway."

Luka whirled around toward Holly. His blue angel eyes sparkled as they boldly caressed every inch of her unclothed body as if to remind her of their shared intimacy. He stepped closer to her as he pulled off his brown leather bomber jacket and let it hit the floor with a thud.

Oh, no. He picks here, and now, to come after me?

Luka stood close, oh, so close. Everything about him made her respond weak and vulnerable. She reached out, and lightly touched his soft and inviting, flannel Asset shirt that was so incredibly blue like his eyes. She hesitantly placed the palm of her hand against his chest, to remember, to prove he was flesh-and-blood. Was she fooling herself? To touch Luka ordered the outside world to vanish.

He stepped closer, and a soft, golden glow spilled onto Luka from the lit wall sconce. His face reflected the gold, shimmering light as it bathed his tanned skin.

She quickly glanced at the sleeves of his blue shirt. One unbuttoned at the wrist. The other half rolled to his elbow, noting he hadn't enough time to dress this morning. His collar was straight, and the top two buttons of his shirt fell open, allowing her a peek at his chest. He was doing it again, sucking her deep into a perfectly delicious, wicked spell that only he wove.

Holly fought her natural reaction to reach over, slip her hand inside the shirt, and caress the creamy, light brown hair on his chest. Instead, she ran her fingertips along the edge of his black leather vest until she reached the bottom. Her hand fell to his hips and then molded to his tight black Levi's hugging him, as she wanted to do. She snagged her index finger in one of his belt loops. A long, expensive, white silk scarf hung loosely around his neck to his waist. Luka Hunter was bewitching her, leaving her mind in a dizzy whirl. He was calling her to him with his electric eyes and then with his sizzling body.

To yield was easy, and she became blindly obedient and gazed deeply into his incredible blue eyes, watching him measure his resistance. But no use, he was lost to the magnetism of her nearness. He was fighting the battle but was losing, and she watched his forgiveness simmer. He was struggling to forget, to make her forget. She saw the darkness shroud his face, he'd remembered, and he squelched the forgiveness that wanted to bubble up, spill over, and tell her nothing matter but her.

It had been too long since she'd touched him. She tried to remember how it was to touch Luka's angel hair, disheveled by the annoying wind and caused her to wonder as she drifted, lost in a dream. Would his golden spun hair look like this when he finished making love? The rims of his eyes looked tired and were lined with dark, threatening circles, but oh, those fucking blue eyes-to-die-for, they were alert, and simmering with ideas because he was looking at her. The tight coil of desire thundered deep within as his eyes studied the first hook on the corset.

Luka moved closer, working his nimble fingers, trying to unfasten the rusty hook on the bottom from the eye. She sighed slightly recalling how his talented fingers brought her so much exquisite pleasure. He tilted his head to get a better look, and his long, golden hair cascaded down his shoulders like sparkling moonlight dancing on the ocean.

"This is all wrong. This lady has a shape. I want it showing," he barked.

"Luka if you want her filmed in authentic costume then...." Lilly advised picking up another corset to show Luka.

"Sorry, you're doing your job, Lil. Forgive me, but I'm looking for a particular image. Go quickly and find me antique lingerie. White if you have it. Tell them on the set it will be another half hour."

Lilly saluted to tease Luka and left.

Holly was reeling.

Alone with Luka.

No, she didn't want to be alone, especially another half hour with her golden angel.

"Give me strength," she begged, hoping that, in another half hour she'd have a choice left.

"You will need more than that to stop me," he murmured under his breath, and then glanced up at her.

The blaze slapped Holly's cheeks.

Luka dropped his gaze, and his fingers moved up hook by hook, unfastening the corset. The pressure of his icy knuckles brushing against her breasts sets off an unexpected chain of explosive hot and cold sensations. There was nowhere to run.

Trapped.

Drowning.

Luka. The crisp, scent of him, awoke her as if she had been in a deep sleep. She closed her eyes and begged again, "Have mercy on me, Luka," barely above a whisper.

"Never." He forewarned.

The depth of his caring shined brightly in the gentle smile he shared with her. Then his warm puffs of breath caressed the tops of her cool breasts, reminding her of their morning's intimate pleasure. She stretched, arching her back, and with her desire on high, dreamed of placing her nipple into his warm, succulent mouth. She turned off her internal warning system sounding loud and clear. Luka's sensual aura commanding presence was overriding any sense of right, and wrong, and something dangerous was about to happen.

Then it did.

Luka dropped his warm, sensuous, lips gently onto the top curve of her breast.

She closed her eyes and shamelessly arched more, seeking his touch as if she would perish without his lips. His warm tongue licked her chest and carved a fiery trail to her shoulders.

He put her on alert.

Her traitorous body trembled and tingled from the titillating sparks of fire that radiated from him. Consumed by the burn, she was barely able to slip in a tiny breath as she plummeted into Luka.

Luka...

Aroused.

That thought brought a wicked smile to her face. This whole incredible experience had begun with Luka, the magic man, her beautiful Luka, who had trusted her. Why, oh why, had she betrayed him?

Luka stopped kissing her at the soft crook of her neck. He straightened and his intense gaze dove deep into hers.

A monstrous craving overcame her that matched the thick black lust in his eyes. They told her she was messing with a dangerous man, a powerful man. Her body shuddered in response, caught in the grips of something so wild and maddening, it compelled her to move her mouth nearer his. She wanted so much to taste him, no matter the price. She wanted nothing more than to sink in the sweet torture of Luka's erotic kiss.

Instead, Luka glanced down to unfasten the last few hooks.

It wasn't exactly what she'd been thinking, but she liked his train of thought. He wanted her naked. However, her long strands of curled hair kept getting in the way.

Luka became downright exasperated with the uncooperative fasteners. He glanced up quickly. His frustration wrapped tightly around the edge of his lips, forcing his eyebrows together.

"Can you hold your hair up so I can fasten the last of these bloody foul hooks?" He said through his teeth.

His masculine scent was potent, driving her to close her eyes again and imagine them locked in each other's arms. Her legs parted a bit as if to invite those magic fingers. She mechanically lifted her hair with both hands, hopelessly lost in a daydream of making love with him.

When Luka unfastened the last hook, her full breasts bounced free launching the wicked corset to the floor with a thud beside his jacket.

Aroused from her daydream, Holly stood stunned.

"Fuck!" He said with restraint.

Out of her peripheral vision, she caught her reflection in the full-length mirror. She wouldn't have thought it possible to be dressed only in a white lace thong, with her dark patch of hair visible through the thin lace panel, inches away from the always beautiful Luka.

Fuck was right.

Luka glanced away and stepped behind her. His eyes testified that he was fighting something wild and untamed in him.

She hoped he would win and take her because the air was so magnetic she could taste the sexual tension. He wanted her badly.

Luka's eyes were committing to memory, every inch of her body.

Holly watched as her full breasts caused him grievous distress. Though she must admit, she enjoyed having an influence on him, and she half expected him to ravish her on the spot. She wanted him to move closer and show her how much his hard driving need ached for her. However, Luka Hunter would never do that. He was always a gentleman first. Holly watched him lock away his private dreams and fantasies for her behind the cloak of a far-away look.

Holly no longer found his sparkling, blue eyes looking back at her. These were guarded eyes. Her flights of imagination quickly sank into a dismal gloom. Luka was punishing her by holding back his thoughts, his emotions, and especially his sensual and scorching touch from her. She bristled and caught her breath because once again, her sensibilities were turned inside out.

This madness has to stop at once!

And she screamed in the dark corridors of her mind. No matter, she couldn't stop her raging cry for pleasure with

Luka. It was running wild as a leaf blowing in a tempestuous wind, causing her to stare at him, lost in him, daring him to touch her. When he wouldn't, she stepped back to test his resolve and pressed the length of her body against Luka.

"Don't ... don't ... do that." He stammered, his voice thick and husky.

His determined reaction made her yearn for him even more. She didn't understand why. What was happening to her? She stood close to Luka, she wanted to throw herself into his arms and plead for his forgiveness. His eyes warned forgiveness was not what she needed from him.

"Luka...." She softly lamented.

Would she ever regain his trust?

Luka took a deep, ragged breath, puffed his chest, and barely brushing her back, touched her ever so lightly.

"Luka...," she repeated, moving slowly to face him.

"I can't do this." He blasted.

Apparently her betrayal weighed so heavy on his mind that it was easier to resist her.

Luka hollered at the top of his lungs. "Lil! Where the fuck are you?" His voice, growing smaller, and smaller. Luka barked again as he glanced down at Holly and promptly made sure to avert his eyes from her breasts. "Lil, blast it, we don't have time for you to search the entire wardrobe! Lil, bring what you have straightaway."

Lilly returned, and handed Luka's outstretched hand a small stack of delicate lace, and satin undergarments.

"Brilliant. Find me a long, snow-white, flowing gown," and then he added, "low cut as the censor's permits."

Lilly's eyes bulged with surprise at the unexpected sight of

Holly dressed only in a thong, and so close to Luka. Lilly whirled on her heel and hurriedly left the room.

Nothing changed. His eyes remained icy blue, and distant — her betrayal with Kaine stood loud and clear between them.

He stepped away from her, holding her at arm's length and took another step back. "You have nothing to worry about from me. I'm here to do the job." Luka maintained with no emotion, his eyes avoiding her nakedness. Then he turned his attention to another corset from Lilly's stack of delicacies. He held the fine cloth like a gentleman, as an expert, rubbing the satin between his fingertips deciding if the texture was tolerable. He tossed the swatch of lace and satin at Holly.

She missed it and bent at the waist to retrieve it. She hoped her provocative pose would entice the always sensual Luka, trapped in a twilight state of arousal. Now, she needed to find the courage to call his bluff, fan his lust until he was in a first stage alert of arousal. He was a lot of man. How wise was it to provoke the animal — Luka, untamed and aroused?

Mmmm.

She would need all her strength.

Somewhere in the last corridor of her reasoning came a slicing bolt of guilt. It struck her hard, sent to fight her traitorous behavior. The fiery feelings for Luka weren't right. Holly lifted her chin, resolved to deny her instinct to rock against him, and instead straighten her spine. She stood, coolly holding the corset. She caught her breasts between her forearms as she watched his eyes follow the sway of them. She had to admit, she'd enjoyed the subtle exchange, and how the seduction had worked putting him right where she wanted him. His hot eyes now followed her every movement. She smiled an understanding smile at him, for they needed no words.

Holly held the moment. Her simple charms were working, and she looked down for the proof of his arousal in his pants. She smiled again. Luka was so flesh-and-blood. She remembered the lingerie in her hands. She liked the looks of this corset. Perhaps it would support her ample breasts instead of crush them. She glanced again at him, noticing his renewed cool, controlled, attitude toward her.

His response miffed her, and she made another decision. Luka Hunter wanted to force himself on her with the weak excuse of helping Lilly. Well, two could play at that game.

Holly straightened her shoulders, flaunting a bit. She pretended her attention was on the corset. She was amazed at how calm and poised she acted standing next to Luka practically naked. The gut-wrenching twists of fire must glow from her. Still, it seemed right, to have his eyes rake over every curve of her body whenever he thought she wasn't looking. She almost felt his intimate thoughts — almost. It seemed her habitual proximity to these sexy Englishmen compelled another sensual personality of hers to the surface. They had revitalized her feminine spirit, drawing out her power and confidence in her own body.

Luka stepped away to inspect something on the gold paper.

Holly's thoughts quietly questioned why Lilly had brought such a beautifully wrapped package.

He smiled a satisfying grin at the contents and then to her. The sparkle had returned, and there was an added touch of expectation. With the grace of holding a cloud, he held up a pair of white, silk stockings draped across his palm.

He stopped — he watched her.

She understood the urgent longing flash in his eyes. Never had a man made love to her with his eyes, only Luka. The deep lusty pools were excited and filled with delicious expectation. The intense passion of Luka was growing stronger. His piercing blue eyes were challenging hers. After a long pause, they unnerved her. All her resolve to seduce him disappeared like smoke. Luka made it perfectly clear. If he maneuvered her this easy with his eyes, in this game, she was way out of her league.

Holly shrugged off his potent glare, assuming Luka had been with hundreds of naked women during his global travels. She quickly became ashamed of her childish prank and felt utterly exposed, standing bare-chested. This impossible man drove her beyond her experience, and even further beyond her sanity. It seemed he wanted her only on his terms. She returned her attention to the corset, but she was too exasperated to work her fingers to lace the hooks. They had become numb from the coolness of the atmosphere. Or, was it because she was lost in a cold set of circumstances.

Her frustration raged, never expecting to find herself naked, this close to Luka, and he would remain detached, stepping behind his thick armor to protect his feelings from her.

"Can you get the bloody thing on?" he asked coolly, breaking the silence.

"No!" She hollered with an edge, surprised that she couldn't lace the old-fashioned corset alone either.

He stood quietly assessing her.

She'd have given him anything to share his thoughts with her.

Finally, he took a begrudging step closer, apparently resigned to assist her.

Her heart raced as he stood within kissing distance. When he'd finished the last hook, he straightened his back, but before he looked away, he locked his gaze onto hers, but only for a fleeting second.

What was it he saw in her eyes to repulse him so to make him turn away so fast?

Chapter Three

PRETTY BALLERINA

L uka stepped behind Holly. He wrapped the corsets' long white ribbons around his hands as if coiling rope while she bent and held on to the post. He pulled the laces until she was sure no more air could rise from her lungs. Her breasts were puffed up so high she rested her chin on them.

"Better." That was all he gave up as he backed up, sat on an old wooden trunk, cocked his head, and lowered his lids. His body relaxed into the silence, but his eyes were fixed, watching her like prey about to pounce. His breathing was even, and deliberate. His beautiful face continued to wear an expression of indifference. His smoky blue eyes were beginning to make it clear. The vision of her pleased him as they roamed over her body.

Then he spoke softly, his comment almost a whisper, "Turn around ... again."

His persuasive requests made her skin tingle, her head, dizzy with dangerous excitement as she slowly turned for him.

"Again, ... again, ... again," he directed under his breath every few moments.

His behavior became apparent as she read Luka's eyes. She was his creation and belonged to him. His hypnotic blue eyes-to-die for glazed as if mesmerized by her, as if she was the only beautiful woman in the world. If he had been any other man, his gaze, so devoted, worshiping her would be of a man falling in love with her.

Was that why she loved to stand on a pedestal dressed in nothing but silk lingerie and turn for Luka like a ballerina in a jewelry box?

It was marvelous to have his steady gaze, watching him dream about him loving and touching her everywhere. The warm rush of heat settled about her cheeks, yet she stood straight with confidence, knowing she pleased him.

She broke the trance and let her eyes drift pleasurably down the length of his sexy body. Her smile told him how gorgeous he was to her. But more about her raw urgency to raise his arousal to the level of the fires of Hell.

When Luka Hunter was aroused, no words adequately describe him when he was like this, eyes glittering, lost in lust, devouring every inch of her, his groin half swollen.

MATTER OF TIME

Luka stood up breaking the silent tension. He walked up behind her, turned her back to him, and stared into the mirror at her. He bowed his head. His soft hair caressed the side of her shoulder and upper arm, as he placed his warm, soft lips upon her shoulder. The tender kiss sent a wave of red-hot heat to the top of her legs. He lightly brushed his fiery lips back and forth over her skin like the wings of a butterfly. Then his voice cut into the dream state to remind her of her betrayal.

"Is he treating you well?"

Holly sighed a defeated tone, lowered her lashes, her elation squashed. She looked away from him, and she didn't answer. To speak of Kaine encouraged feelings of depravity, and she didn't like them. It was as if Luka was reminding her where her loyalties should be, certainly not there trying to seduce him.

She fought to keep her gaze averted, but Luka's proximity caused her bones to dissolve to liquid. Had he decided to forgive her? She wanted to test to see, so she stepped back into his solid, warm body, leaning on him, molding his thick hardness into her lower back. She swept her gaze up into the mirror to find him lock on to her. She closed her eyes to succumb to the hot, lusty feelings that swept over her like a prairie fire in the dry brush, extinguishing her betrayal. She opened them.

He seemed to be weakening.

Luka was finally under the spell of the enchanting castle and he took another long, leisurely visual trip up, and down her body then locked onto her eyes again, leaning in a bit to allow his hot cheek to rest on hers. He was dropping his armor, showing her he was still interested. The soft light from the sconce followed the contour of his perfect features, dusting them with shimmering gold. He was a new creation. Someone, she'd never seen.

Mmmm, Luka.

He reached around and touched her belly with the cool pads of his fingertips so gently the shock waves were almost unbearable. He had forgiven her and was allowing Holly his magic touch as he slid his hands across her stomach, and up the ladder of her midriff. His hands moved quickly to the base of her breasts and cupped them as if his possessions, running his thumbs lightly over the sheer layer of lace. Her nipples hardened as he stroked her sensitive peak purposefully bringing another fiery bolt of passion rendering her weak-kneed. The longer Luka touched her, the more his eyes softened, his heart was trying to trust her.

With the worst behind them, Holly twisted in his familiar embrace sliding her hands up to dig her fingers deep into his silky hair. She was about to kiss him senseless when Luka cautioned.

"I'm not your problem. It's Kaine. You need to be careful. After you spend time with him, you will look over your shoulder wondering where I am."

His words were like a bucket of ice thrown on her, meant to squelch her hot, erotic plans for him. Raw agony throbbed in her veins, as he placed his warm, smooth cheek next to her again. It forced her to close her eyes to steady herself, to hold back the flood of hot tears because his painful rejection was hard to bear. She lifted her chin to face him trying to bring calm to her words.

"Please, Luka. Kaine is not a problem. I am," she explained and then dropped her arms from around his shoulders to rest on his forearms.

He did not put his hands around her waist and would not hold her or lavish her with the wicked sensations she wanted from him. He'd raised the impenetrable shield once again, and became lost to her.

She stood awkwardly filled with disappointment and regret.

"I'm, so sorry. I never expected things to work out as they have. I'd given anything not to have hurt you."

Luka stepped back and looked down to pin her eyes. They narrowed as if she had insulted him. He raised his arms harshly to break her hold on him. He flicked his golden hair back over his shoulder with agitation and declared with a heavy dose of irritation.

"You haven't hurt me. To hurt me, I have to lose you. As you can see, I don't look worried. I can tell by your willingness to please me that I haven't lost you, on the contrary, so far I have the advantage. You see, I know Kaine, and you don't. However, for the record, I'll be nearby. It's only a matter of time."

Luka's confident attitude infuriated her. What made him so damn cocksure about her? Well, she would show him!

To calm herself she responded with a soothing tone above a whisper. "Please, don't speak this way about Kaine."

"Then I won't. I'll speak about me. I want you to believe me. One day soon, you will look at me the way you did, the way you look at Kaine now."

"How is it I look at Kaine?"

"You look at him with eyes that adore him."

Holly remembered when Kaine said those same words about her and Luka, in the cab on their way out to go sightseeing.

What she saw in Luka's eyes was a pinkish tint, for a split second. Then he stepped back again and briskly glanced away. The silence rushed in to crush her.

The two words trailed.

Adore him....

No longer concerned about anything other than this spectacular man she dropped her head as if bushwhacked then left for dead. She'd misunderstood. Luka hadn't been punishing her by withdrawing his touch. He had been warring with himself, knowing Kaine had replaced him in her eyes, in her heart — in bed.

He'd read the headlines.

She'd become the secret girlfriend. He'd sent into Kaine's arms. Now, he professed to be waiting for her because he wanted her. He'd wait, knowing Kaine would blow his chance.

At that moment, Lilly burst into the tiny room. She cleared throat to announce herself and then quickly averted her eyes. She glanced at Holly with eyes full of questions she dared not ask.

Meanwhile, Luka returned to loop the ribbons on her corset and tied them in a bow at the bottom.

To Holly's surprise, he boldly placed his warm hands on her, running them to her breasts, brazenly settling his palms over her curves as he adjusted the corset to his liking. He deliberately brushed his thumbs against her pebble hard nipples, over and over again, driving her to irrationality. He smiled his sexy boyish smile to let her see he enjoyed the exchange, his hands pushed, and prodded her breasts to prop them up higher.

Lilly handed him the oil, and he started the torture once more, roaming her body freely, spreading the shimmering lavender scented body moisturizer. He moved gracefully with the complete freedom of her lover, as he made the only love to her he could, and he felt good, better than good, perfect.

The oil was incandescent to make her skin glow for the camera, but the touch of his fingers did that. He continued to move his soft hand on the inside of her leg to the top of her thighs leaving her wet and wanting. The burn, oh, ached so much. The savage heat was burning her alive, and Luka wouldn't do a thing but rejoiced in his success.

He wouldn't quit.

He offered a pair of beautiful stockings to put on then he purposely smoothed them high up on her thigh, so careful, not to leave any wrinkles. Next Holly stepped into first one garter, and then the other that he held for her and slipped them one at a time up her thighs to hold the softest silk stockings. She pondered if Rumpelstiltskin had spun these for her legs alone.

Luka left an aching trail of longing on her skin wherever he touched her. Her only impulse was to drop to the floor, rip his clothes from his virile body, and then run her hands over his naked body, tasting every inch of his flesh.

She made sure he saw the raging need in her eyes. She had no intention of hiding how irrational, he made her feel.

Luka remained cool, controlled, and matter-of-fact. He was a master and a gentleman. He had a job to finish. He circled her like a cat as he held up a low-cut, pearl-white, lace dress high above her head. He made sure it didn't disturb her hair as he draped it down over her plump breasts. Luka was creating her again, especially for him. When he'd finished marking his territory, his possession, her body ached for only him.

Okay, Mr. Hunter, you can put your hands all over me. Drive me beyond the limits of my sanity while I can't even quicken your breath. Who the hell are you?

Luka sat back down on the trunk, crossed his arms over his chest, kicked his long legs out in front of him, and crossed them at the ankle. He threw his head back, taking a long look at Holly as if an artist evaluating his work, cocking his head from one side to the other. He sat up and called Lilly to him. He whispered something, and she left with haste.

"Turn for me. I have to imagine all of you." He directed.

Wow, how did a girl respond to a request like that?

Thankfully, Lilly took the surprise out of his heady request when she quickly returned and hurried toward Luka. She clutched something small in her hands.

He got up, took Holly's arm, and helped her down the pedestal and led her over to the trunk where he offered her a seat. He bent down on one knee. His golden hair fell forward as he picked up her heel and slipped a pair of silver ballerina slippers onto each foot. She bit down on her lip and cursed herself for being impatient. Would he ever let up impressing her?

Peter arrived next and after he had finished with her makeup, he'd left. She'd become Luka's vision of purity and chastity, far from his vision of her as the sensual seductress, dripping with black lace at the Hard Rock.

Every man's wicked dream ... he'd said.

Lilly quietly picked up the discarded costume pieces and left.

Alone again, with Luka.

Holly wasn't sure she possessed the strength to be alone with her angel eyes man any longer. It had been so difficult to keep from making a complete fool of herself when his hands ran rampant over her flesh, teaching every inch of her to hunger for his special touch.

He sat back and pulled his knee up to rest his elbow, his hand curled under his chin.

She sensed the weight of his steady stare as his eyes always seemed to undress her, daring her to stop him from gazing deeply into her soul. She felt more naked with him now because he seemed as if he intuited things about her before she did.

How could he?

She decided to ask him. "How will this story end Luka?"

He choked back a smile, flipped back a long strand of hair.

"Simple. You and I will watch a thousand sunsets."

His quiet answer hung frozen, suspended in time.

So many words she wanted to say like the promises she and Kaine made to each other. Instead, she was drawn inches from him. She dropped down on haunches. She was close, so close to explaining the morning with Kaine. Her index finger curled a strand of his long, angel hair. With her fingertip, she traced the line of his face from his sideburn to his chin. The simple gesture of affection melted her into a pool of lusty quicksilver for him to mold any way he wanted

It must have done the same to him because as her fingers traveled halfway down his face, he caught her hand. He pressed her palm against the side of his cheek, and she watched him fight himself not to nestle into it. His eyes never lied. He longed for her badly. His eyes said he fought to stop himself from showing her all the pleasure she wanted from him, but was trapped in an impossible set of circumstances.

She sighed as her throat clogged with words she dared not speak. She squeezed his hand meaningfully, the same hand that had ravished her, the hand that had touched her with tenderness, and fire. She moved to her knees, closer to his face. She was a breath away from his lips. It looked like he was going to kiss her because he closed his beautiful blue eyes. To lose Luka was an extraordinarily high price to pay to stay with Kaine.

"Well, isn't this a tender scene?" Kaine's icy voice blasted. The poisonous look in his eyes pinned Luka.

Holly jumped, falling forward into Luka's arms, Kaine's untimely arrival. She twisted her neck and looked up to see he lit up the room. Kaine, her rock star Prince, though he looked more like a lost, romantic time-traveler from King Arthur's court. His dark, shiny hair pulled back behind his head showing off his long sideburns. A twelfth-century costume covered the chest, she loved to caress with a dove white, gauzy shirt with long willowy sleeves. Wrapped around his neck, and wrists were thick jewel toned costume jewelry that glistened. Draped over Kaine's masculine shoulders hung a floor-length, black velvet cloak with a high crimson collar. He stood in his rock 'n' roll black leather pants, and black boots, that whirled around and stormed out of the room.

Chapter Five

NEVER TEAR US APART

L uka chortled loudly so Kaine would hear him in the hallway. "Prince Charming isn't having a marvelous day?"

Before Holly decided which direction to go, Luka surrounded her with his embrace, pulling her up and over his legs to straddle his lap. With one sweeping movement of his hand, he encircled the back of her head ever so gently, but firmly. He wove his fingers into her long curled locks, pulling her into him. His tongue entered her open mouth so swiftly she had no time to think.

She surrendered quickly to his passionate strokes, again, and again, and again. His powerful tongue continued to mark the inside of her mouth, burning her with his dangerous passion. He was expressing his misery without her. How each second, he was burning in Hell knowing she was with Kaine.

Luka put her on notice that, without any doubt, she was his. She was Luka's Lady. He kissed her so quickly and deeply she simply never thought to move away because her body yielded, so willing to fill the folds of his body. At that moment, he became her moon, her sun, her universe. She longed for him, cared for him, adored him — yet — being with him like this was wrong. Regardless, she returned the kiss with an unquestionable inevitability that bound her to him, and him, alone. She didn't want him to stop kissing her as she pressed her breasts into his chest, pushed her hips to fit snugly over his swelling groin. She was so ready for him.

But Luka wouldn't give all of himself to her.

With her gown hiked up to her thighs, she wrapped her legs around his waist.

It was too late.

Luka pulled away ready to release her. He held her limp body tightly until she regained her balance. She noted the smugness lacing his icy blue eyes. A lazy, sexy smile had pressed at the corners of his lips before he challenged her.

"See? I make you forget Kaine, and you don't like that? Do you?"

Chapter Six

BEFORE YOU ACCUSE ME

His assessment was accurate. She'd never tell him now. His arrogance had pressed the wrong button, pushing her too far. She looked straight in his self-righteous blue eyes and declared.

"I will never forget Kaine. Never! Consider that a goodbye kiss."

A little part of her died inside because she deceived him. Ashamed of her sexy performance with Luka, Holly attempted to ignore the truth of his observation.

She motioned with her head toward the door, to refer to Kaine's hasty retreat. She scolded. "Now, look what *you* have done."

She whirled around to run toward the arched doorway to catch up with Kaine.

However, he surprised her again and tightly gripped her elbow.

"That hurts!" She complained.

Only Luka didn't relax his grip. He stood holding her

tighter, pulling her so close to his body. His masculine heat scalded her. His arms surrounded her waist as he reeled her in so close. He held her, his prisoner as if unable to let her go. His heart pounded reflecting the strain of this horrible situation and clouded the usual glow in his eyes.

He flicked his long golden hair behind him with his head, and his hand came up to her throat, and he gripped her chin, pulling her a breath away from him. His eyes challenged her.

"You see? Your peacock lover would rather believe I am guilty of tempting you to ease his guilty conscience. That I have compromised you, instead of him. He's tried to take you from me, and now he refuses to trust his gut.

"The truth is, after the night with him, you can't forget me, and you want me. I didn't force you to stay in the dressing room with me. I didn't force you to enjoy my touch as I caressed all of your beautiful body. You never resisted my kisses, my touch. You can't. I know it, and now, you know. Your body recognizes my touch. It will never forget me. Your eyes shine because of *my* touch. These kisses aren't goodbye. I think I might take one more liberty with you, and enjoy what it is that Kaine will bloody well accuse me of doing."

Holly struggled to free herself from his restraint. She didn't need any more of Luka's truths. However, he wasn't prepared to let her run back to Kaine. His hand held her face so close to his, all the while, his cool, blue eyes were telling her. Go ahead, run to Kaine, but she was his.

Holly's body responded as willingly as Luka predicted. His skilled hand ran up, and down her back, touching her in all the places she loved. She was melting against him. He was imposing her sentence, and as if to seal a pact with the Devil, he dropped his hot mouth upon her lips again.

She surrendered, tilting her head back to soak up the moistness of his lips with no hesitation.

He touched her everywhere he wanted, leaving her limp and breathless. Then he broke the magic moment and spoke a breath away from her mouth.

"Kaine's jealousy will destroy any possible feelings he might misconstrue as love for you because he is incapable of real love. So, go if you don't believe me. Run to him. Kiss and make-up or this shoot will become bloody hell, putting up with his sulkiness. I can trust you to bring him out of his tailspin."

She moved again to break his stifling embrace, but he was not finished. He brought his lips down, crashing on her again, kissing her to oblivion.

The self-righteousness of Luka's last remark seeped in and slapped her pride vigorously, bringing her to her senses. She was flushed with arousal and struggling for breath when Luka decided to release her.

Fighting mad, instead of staying to argue with him, she pried herself from his enslaving grasp.

"You're so wrong, the kiss *was* goodbye." She picked up the front of her long, white, gown and fled from the room, never looking back.

Holly's eyes were blazing with hot tears as she blundered into the inky darkness of the corridor. She blotted more stinging tears with the back of her other hand, gingerly trying not to smear her makeup. More hot tears followed angry tears. Why did he dismiss her and mock her by setting her free to run to Kaine? That thought was laced with black despair and burned up her confidence. She was so afraid Luka knew her better than she knew herself.

Can't forget me. Still want me.

His words echoed in her mind.

She hoped Luka was wrong in his evaluation of the situation because then she was running in the wrong direction. It should be to him — not to Kaine.

Where was Kaine?

She died a little inside because she'd also deceived Kaine. It was imperative that she find him to explain. But explain what? That Luka holding her so intimately wasn't how it looked. She wasn't consistently attracted to Luka as Kaine thought. Luka thought. Hell, everyone thought.

"Damn!" She swore aloud cursing the situation, carrying the front of the maiden's gown in her hands as she hurried along the long, dark corridor cursing herself. Why hadn't she resisted Luka's magician's spell?

Oh, how he'd kiss her, to oblivion, after Kaine's disillusioned reaction. She'd never met a man as complicated as Luka Hunter. And that delicious look in his eyes. Oh, hell, say it, the longing for her he had in such a passionate and irrational way. He always wanted to touch her, to kiss her, but then wouldn't, and stops.

But other times, he would lose the war with himself and kiss her with his knee-bending, loin-moistening, heart-pounding, breathless kisses.

He was right.

Luka Hunter was showing her no mercy.

Chapter Seven

CAN'T STAND IT

Holly couldn't release the blaze of sensual thoughts after Luka's persuasive kisses. Or, his words so even toned and resolved.

It's a matter of time.

She spotted Kaine up ahead.

"Kaine, please, wait. Kaine?"

She hurried along the narrow, dark, and musty corridor, cursing herself again aloud for being so inexperienced. But how in the world would she anticipate these two powerhouse men fighting over her like the last sweet in the candy shop?

"Kaine, Kaine," she called out hearing an immediate echo. His faint shadow was preparing to exit the castle corridor, so she hurried with her head full of unsatisfactory explanations. She closed her eyes for a split second. She had to forget Luka, quick.

As Holly arrived at Kaine's side, she'd decided to tell the truth, and blurted.

"I'm, so sorry. It was exactly what it looked like. Luka

crossed the line, and I didn't stop him. My emotions and good sense evaporate when I'm close to him. I've told him goodbye, and I promise it won't happen again."

She'd told Luka goodbye, but now wasn't the time to mention she had encouraged his advances, had been rejected and then sent to cool Kaine's jealousy. Her words didn't seem to influence Kaine either.

With a chilly, detached expression, he admitted as if annoyed, "I appreciate your honesty. We have nothing if we don't have that."

He warmed up a bit to her. "I'm glad I didn't have to point that out. However, you're essentially wrong. It will happen again, and again. Luka will keep coming after you. But, I don't blame you because you're far too trusting and look for the good in others. You must watch out for Luka. He won't stop undermining me until he has what he desires. And that My Lady is you. So please, don't think I don't understand, I do, far too well. I know him better than he does."

Kaine's assertive tone caused her to back up feeling ill at ease.

"That's funny. Luka said the same about you." She volunteered.

"This is not funny," Kaine, stated flatly, his voice cold, as the words poured forth through clenched teeth.

She stopped grinning.

He added, "Holly, obviously it hasn't occurred to you. That even though you and I recently met and have talked about making this relationship work, to those that count, you're *my* girlfriend. But a few minutes ago, I found you in Luka's arms. Do you understand all the implications of that? I'm doing my best to understand because I know Luka and he is deadly serious about you and will eventually pull out all the stops. Ask anyone. He's behaving differently. It's because of you. Stay close to me, Holly. I don't want to lose you to him because you think Luka plays fair — he doesn't.

"You're my *girlfriend*. I take that word incredibly serious and all that comes with it because I care about you. But being with Luka in compromising situations does have a limit. I'm not paranoid. I have years of experience in these types of circumstances with him. But never have the stakes been this high, the future with you.

"If you had never met Luka, you and I would be facing a brilliant, happy life. I am confident that I can make you happy, give you everything a woman wants. I'd relax, and let time take care of our love. But that is not what happened, is it? We have Luka to contend with, and Holly, so you're clear, he is the only man that has as much as I do, to offer you. He has his looks, charm, and other talents, but his greatest power is your attraction to him.

"I'm keenly aware of what I'm up against with Luka. You, My Lady, don't, and are the weak link because he can so easily influence you. Think about it, you're my girlfriend, and he's proven that he not only can seduce you but also able to flaunt it in my face. That tells both of us he can bide his time. He's counting on my being out of the way the next eighteen months, because I'm committed to the tour, and he's leaving in a week. It is damn near impossible to sustain a relationship when I'm off the road, but the harsh and constant pressures of a worldwide tour can prove too much for you and me. He will wait and watch you. And that eats me up inside here." He said while pounding on his chest.

Kaine took her in his trembling arms and held her tight until he forgot all of his warnings against Luka. He looked down at her, and his eyes shimmered with a new expectation. His words flowed into her ear as a feather floating on a wispy wind. "Look at you, My Lady Fair. Here I am going on about my nemesis when you're a perfect vision. More enchanting than any woman I've ever seen," and then he sighed as if defeated, releasing the warm breath.

The sweetness of him kissed her face and sent a barrage of tingling sensations through her body as his masculine cologne rushed her senses.

She barely managed to say. "I'm, so sorry, that I've disappointed you," as she ran Kaine's indicting words around in her mind as if on a loop.

You're *my girlfriend.*

I found you in Luka's arms.

There is a limit!

As soon as she had some free time, she was going to have to sort out his remarks.

Did she cheat on Kaine with Luka?

In the next moment, the distance between them caused by Luka vanished, and both were lost in the magic they made together. The fairy tale characters stood as if they shared the same skin.

Unfortunately, it was short lived.

Luka coolly walked up behind them, bringing with him a brittle chill, colder than a blast of the northern winds in winter, and it spread quickly between the two men.

"Hey mate," Luka called out to Kaine as cheerful as if

speaking to an old time war buddy.

"Haven't I dressed our Holly as every chap's dream?" He boasted, rubbing it in, emphasizing the word *our,* and then paused to glare at Kaine as if he were waiting for a dramatic response from the effect of his choice of words.

However, Kaine stood silent.

Surprisingly, Luka backed away throwing his hands in the air.

"Okay ... my dream." He shifted his weight to his other foot.

"You approve of the costume I've selected? Do you like how the gown cascades around her to accentuate every curve, every fold, and crease of her body? She's my finest work, the manifestation of an innocent maiden. This lady could sell the apple back to the snake. Don't you agree, Governor?" Luka baited.

Kaine's facial muscles were becoming more taut and tight and Holly heard his teeth grinding at the back of his jaw.

Clearly, Luka didn't want Kaine's opinion as he continued to speak. "I can't stop admiring her, don't you agree Kaine? She is exactly ... no, I'll say it here, and now. She *is* the woman I've dreamed of, the one, the *only* woman I want."

Luka let his statement settle in to irritate Kaine.

He added, "Angelic, but willing enough to invite me to touch her anywhere I want, whenever I want."

Holly was tongue-tied by Luka's ill-mannered declaration, so unlike him. She immediately understood Kaine's concerns for her future with these two men. She was Kaine's girlfriend, and Luka had no business saying those provocative words aloud, even if he believed them. Words laced with impertinence and disrespect. She felt especially uncomfortable.

But Kaine held his emotions intact taking the high road, except for the throwaway glance to Luka that promised that he would never take her from him.

What he said was. "Luka I'm close to shutting your filthy mouth with my fist, but with Holly here, I don't have that luxury. You need to accept that the lady and I have decided to honor the headlines. Miss Hill is *my* girlfriend, so all that is left for you is to dream about her." His tone controlled through clenched teeth, but he squeezed Holly's hand so tightly she was afraid if he lets go it would find its way into Luka's arrogant mouth.

Luka ignored Kaine's territorial markings, stepping closer, daring to take Holly into his arms. Luka laughed lightly, and then heartily. He moved away yelling back as he flicked his long golden hair over his shoulder.

"Okay, I give Gov, for now. Let's go outside before we lose more light. Where is the crew?" He demanded as if nothing important transpired.

Holly adjusted her hand to squeeze Kaine's and forced a temperate smile as she followed him outside the castle.

She hoped this trying day would end soon and commence to honor her new commitment to Kaine. She certainly didn't want to create another nasty confrontation between the testosterone twins. She'd read the message loud and clear in Luka's eyes. He was cool, but Kaine's observations about Luka were correct. She was happy that Kaine had cleared up any confusion there might be, by anyone, especially Luka. The headline was true — she was his girlfriend.

No matter, Luka was waiting.

Meanwhile, Kaine was smoldering with anger as he led Holly over to the white fantasy charger the hero always rode. He dropped her hand. He threw himself up onto the horse's bare back with the ease of a long time ranch hand, sat up straight, appearing handsome as any A-list movie star. He grasped the reins of the red bridle and backed the horse up to a stool, ready to assist Holly's mount behind him.

However, it was time to show Kaine what she had learned in the backcountry of her hometown of Santa Barbara, where she rode with Brett on his thoroughbred horses. She hiked up her dress high in front of her and grabbed firmly onto Kaine's forearm. She stepped on his boot and ignoring the stool, hauled herself up behind him.

"Where did you learn that?" he asked with a satisfied grin.

"You don't have to teach me everything," she retorted arranging her body to sit sidesaddle. It wasn't long before she was shivering in the cold, thick mist. During takes, she had Kaine's hot body to block the biting cold breeze and provided her warmth. Between takes, a warm, plump, down comforter was wrapped around her, but its heat didn't replace Kaine.

Black, ominous, clouds sent sporadic signals of a promised storm that forced Luka to push everyone harder and harder to finish until there was no downtime. For the next few hours, the pace was grueling, and Holly was becoming tired. Not enough sleep and the draining effects of the continual excitement were catching up with her. There had been too many shots, too many stolen kisses from Kaine, a few for the camera, others for himself and too many for Luka. Each kiss, more intense, more insistent. Kaine had her fragile emotions dangling on the edge, placing her in dire need of an emotional rescue.

How much longer would Luka push them? What was he looking to accomplish?

Problems with camera angles had Holly kissing Kaine again, and again, and again. Sometimes she would look to Luka.

See Luka, I can do this. I can.

Why had his confident attitude infuriated her? His only crime was to want her too — because he was arrogant.

As the end of the shoot became increasingly apparent, Luka directed Holly to lean on Kaine's back. She sighed and spoke aloud, half in thought, half in a daydream.

"I'll be sorry to see this fairy tale fantasy end. I wish for you, and I, to go on, here, like this forever."

Kaine acknowledged her comment by squeezing her hand that rested on his thigh. The ever-increasing magic of his touch revived her a bit.

Then Luka called out in an apathetic, hoarse voice. "Last take, okay ... great, come on, smile ... smashing! We're done. That's a wrap."

Kaine slid down first.

"*Mmmm.* Great to stretch."

Kaine stood close to the horse, placed his hands on Holly's waist, and encouraged her to slide down the front of his body, like at the Hard Rock Cafe. Kaine brushed her neck with his full, warm lips.

By the time, she touched the ground, Holly's love struck eyes met Kaine's, shining brightly at the sight of her.

As usual, they wanted each other badly.

Luka's witness to their seemingly isolated demonstration of

affection forced a demanding retort. "The pair of you need to give it a bloody rest!" He blasted as he stomped off heading for the castle.

Kaine moved away from her quickly. In a tone of friendship, he called out loudly to Luka. "Wait up, mate." Kaine looked over to a puzzled Holly and stated. "I'll be back soon."

After excused himself, Kaine sprinted off to catch up with Luka, who had not slowed his gait.

Kaine surprised her once again, by displaying no anger or animosity in his tone of voice toward Luka. The relationship between these two men seemed odd at best, hot one second, cold the next.

That was when Lilly walked up to Holly.

"I have a soft seat and a warm, thick blanket."

After a pause. "And friendship with answers."

Was what Holly was thinking that obvious? However, with any luck, Lilly would clear up a fair amount of the mysteries.

Lilly sat beside Holly, offered her another cup of hot tea, and then explained.

"Take it easy, luv. They're bloody hard to understand. They have lived a life envied by everyone, and they have achieved it as a team. Kaine and Luka grew up together on the road. They have traipsed around the world getting into one scrape after another, loving every minute. And there have been many low times when they were all the family either had. They are closer to me than my own two brothers are because I've toured with *Hurrikaine,* twice. It's always the same story. What one has the other wants."

Holly forced a small smile. "I hope you're wrong. Kaine

says he's willing to build a relationship, but Luka is hell-bent on destroying it. Are you hinting that I have unknowingly become their pawn, to pull first one way, and then the other, as a result of a dreadful game?" Holly inquired, holding back despair as she dropped her head into her hands.

"I didn't mean to upset you. I don't believe that's what's happening at all. This situation is dangerous and not a game. I think they have been on a collision course since they met. This battle was bound to happen someday. The day they found one woman, they both wanted, for the rest of their days and nights. Unfortunately, the day has arrived, and it's *you* they both want.

"Oh, they have shared and passed countless women between them and played horrible, nasty games with women. But nothing like this has ever happened. Each of them seems to be playing for keeps. And I'm concerned because I've grown close to both of them. I love them, and no matter who wins, someone will be injured, and badly. I'm not afraid to say I'm worried about all of you." She laid a comforting hand on Holly's forearm and added, "Be careful. Be sure. Make a decision and then stick to it."

Holly listened with intense interest and then explained. "I have. The choice is made. The headlines call me Kaine's girlfriend, and he is pleased, and so am I. The dressing room? Well, it was the first time I had seen Luka since our decision. I was saying goodbye to him," Holly continued, trying to convince Lilly as well as herself that she was not another game-playing bitch.

"I'll pass on another piece of advice," Lilly offered with the care of a close confidant.

"Please, I need all the perspective I can get."

"This needs repeating. You've chosen Kaine, stay with him because it's far more dangerous to bounce between them," Lilly warned. Then she produced a tiny sympathetic smile as she squeezed Holly's arm. "I don't envy you. Both of them are powerful, sexy, devastatingly handsome men, with wealth beyond reason. I would never want to be in your position."

Chapter Eight

THIS IS LOVE

That was the problem — wasn't it? The clouds hid the sun for too long, and the air was icy cold, sending shivers through her bones. The words circled her head like on a carousel.

Dangerous.

Like, brothers.

Luka had a limit.

You're my girlfriend.

Girlfriend.

The only woman I want.

Holly pulled her knees up under the toasty blanket, so much to think about, so little time. Luckily, the chilling confrontation drifted into the back passages of her thoughts as Luka stepped out of a darkened doorway in the castle. He called to her through a megaphone as he walked toward her like a vision out of a beautiful dream.

"Holly, please, come here," he asked, so soft in tone, no command.

Her body sensed him calling her to him first, and when her mind had caught up, she obeyed. She hadn't taken a few steps before stopping. Kaine stood behind Luka, waiting for her. She didn't like the looks of this. She took another cautious step and then another. She hesitantly approached the two, who for the moment seemed to have buried the hatchet, though, in which back was still a mystery. Still, it seemed they'd agreed to a cease-fire. For that, she was grateful.

"Come with me lovely lady." Luka invited in an octave above a whisper. "I've something to show you," he teased, his cool blue eyes laced with an 'I dare you' attitude.

An uneasy sigh passed from Holly as she glanced to see her rocker, Prince.

Kaine walked up inches behind Luka.

"It's all right. Go with him," Kaine encouraged. He slapped Luka on the upper arm playfully, flashed a weak smile toward Holly, and added, "I have pressing business."

She was, even more, confused. Ready to delivered her prepared statement on being Kaine's woman and set to put her new plan of staying away from Luka to practice, he took her hand and led her away. She wondered if she should follow or stop. So she stopped dead in her tracks.

"I'll behave myself," Luka promised and chuckled while he pulled her alongside him.

She glanced over her right shoulder to see Kaine approaching a beautiful woman. She was elegantly dressed in a dark tweed pantsuit, with shiny, reddish-brown hair, that fell straight to her waist. She judged by how warmly he embraced the woman they were well acquainted even kissed her lightly on the lips. Then he placed his arm around her shoulders companionably and walked in the opposite direction of the video crew.

Holly controlled a strong urge to scratch the woman's eyes out. Then she caught herself and rationalized that the woman must be an old friend, and she turned away.

Luka scoffed, "Don't let Solange get to you. That color of green isn't attractive." Luka's tone of voice changed and sounded as if he was taunting her.

Holly ignored his sully remark as he continued to pull her alongside him, close, too close. She tried not to focus on his intense magnetism while pointing out. "Solange? What a beautiful name," with more enthusiasm than needed.

Luka's silence made it clear he wasn't going to bite and tell her about this Solange.

He laughed, put on his sunniest smile, and informed her.

"You'll have to work for that information. Give me a kiss, and maybe I'll tell you."

"Humph!" She mumbled.

Right now, she wasn't going to give Luka the satisfaction of seeing her jealous. She hoped Kaine would behave better with Solange than she had with Luka.

She studied Luka as he tugged on her hand. She saw he'd grown to care for her. He'd no way to hide it in his eyes. She gave in reluctantly. Kaine would do as he wished.

Luka guided her closer to the castle. She needed to find even ground with him since he was right here. There would be no true goodbyes because he was not going to go away. She stood oh so close to him at the narrow entrance to the castle.

He dropped her hand. He wrapped his arm around her waist.

"You're bloody chilled. Here, let me warm you up a bit."
He volunteered, no suggestion, his voice filled with concern as
his warm, familiar, male body held her companionably.

"I have something to show you. Come with me."

"Not another headline, I hope." She teased but saw the hurt
flash in his eyes at her painful reminder that according to the
media, she was Kaine's mystery girlfriend.

"Better." Luka shot back in a tone that affirmed he'd
instantly forgiven her

He led her through a maze of corridors, up and down stairs
until she was lost with no sense of direction. At the final stage
of a long hallway, she cautiously followed Luka into a dark
room. A tiny light revealed a control booth. Ah, a recording
studio tucked away in the castle. Luka offered her a stool. He
picked up a black cartridge and popped it into the mouth of a
VCR. Seconds later a large black and white image of her
splashed across a wide screen.

She watched on in amazement.

The film showed a close up of Holly's eyes beginning to
close, seducing the camera. Slowly, the camera pulled away
and cut to a full-face shot. Her hair had blown against her
cheek moments before a light mist surrounded her. The eye of
the camera circled her head as Holly waited alone in the mist.
She remembered, she had been waiting for Kaine. Then
magically he appeared as a silhouette. Kaine placed his
incredibly handsome face next to her hair.

Holly's heart pounded as loudly as it had at the Hard Rock
Cafe. Thrilled beyond comment with her portrayal, she
watched the image of her close her eyes again. She was
impressed with Luka's management of the blended, editing

techniques. He'd been hard at work while she was out making headlines. She watched Kaine pause. In the excruciatingly slow motion, she watched him kiss her. Her heart jumped into her throat, it was the fucking kiss of the century. "How magical and surreal they are," she complimented as if she had nothing to do with the images kissing on the screen.

"You're bloody spot on about that."

Holly couldn't break her concentration to comment any further to Luka. The motion of grace with which she filled Kaine's arms astonished her. Holly blushed all over again at her boldness with Kaine, at that time, a total stranger.

Luka spoke up again. "This is brilliant, better than I envisioned. Look at the smoldering and sparkling chemistry brewing between the pair of you. And because you're a born actress, I anticipate today's footage will be as provocative. Watch. Here's my favorite shot." Luka rewound the tape, and replayed the kiss, then slowed the speed to frame-by-frame. "Smashing. Watch the tight closeup on your full, kissable lips."

He stopped and suddenly spun on his heels to face her.

She couldn't help but look at him.

"Lips I want to kiss."

He let the moment sink in and flicked a strand of golden hair across his shoulder then continued his assessment.

"The slow speed builds the excitement until the viewer can't wait for your lips to meet. Men all over the planet are going to dream of sleeping with you, not to mention millions of women are going to be dreaming about being you, Babe."

After his flattering critique, Luka stepped closer to her. His beautiful blue eyes, both red and worn, his eyelids drooped, he looked so tired, but the joy in his eyes from looking at her was fighting to remain. However, seconds later, he'd lost and replaced his joy with a mysterious sadness.

He moved closer.

He was too close to her.

Too, close for keeping her focus.

He leaned beside her ear, and he predicted in a faint whisper.

"One of these days you will be kissing me again like that."

Chapter Nine

CLOSE TO YOU

Day 3

Holly wouldn't look at Luka, especially after Kaine's strong warnings. Luka's words were so powerful, so hopeless. She rose up from the stool and leaned on the recording board's console to steady her body. The heady images flickered on the screen in black and white patterns mesmerizing the audience, because the man and woman fit together so perfectly, as if star-crossed lovers. In a flash, the celluloid illusion vanished, and when Holly looked for Luka, he'd disappeared. A white screen stared back at Holly, daring her to find Luka to ask for a repeat of her provocative performance with Kaine.

Alone with her thoughts, Holly realized what the problem was with Luka's critique. What had occurred between her and Kaine at the Hard Rock Cafe, was not acting on either's part. It had been more of a cold reading, unrehearsed, unexpected, and then unknown. The star-crossed lovers were naturals.

In what manner was it possible that the passionate woman she watched kiss a man she'd never laid eyes on, except with her heart and soul — was her? The woman — so beautiful. Luka's choice of makeup, hair, and wardrobe perfect, and she had met his expectations. The black, lace dress with the mist skirting the floor, coupled with the cinematic theme of film noir, appeared tastefully seductive, perfect. Luka made her beautiful. But no matter how much she admired Luka's image of her, Kaine was the one that showed the world she was desirable above all others.

As if on cue, a gentle breeze found its way into the control booth carrying Kaine's seductive scent. So strong the fragrance, she wondered if the image on the screen had provoked the scent of him — no because now, the warm, full length, of his body closed in from behind her.

Kaine gently pressed his body along the back of hers. Oh, yes, a perfect fit. Another exhausting rush of liquid fire flowed to her cheeks, and then down her body. Kaine pressed his hips into her, making Holly blissfully aware of his arousal, touching her with the lightness of a feather, so close, so persuasive.

Kaine clasped her hand and urged her to follow him over to a dimly lit corner of the control booth where an overstuffed, black leather couch waited.

She looked up into her leading man's dreamy blue eyes. Would her gorgeous rock star prince kiss her? He bent as if to whisper something, but then instead, he playfully pressed a frantic kiss on her lips and spoke into her mouth as he pulled her down onto the couch.

"You, My Lady, are making me crazy." His body quaked with a labored breath. "I can't keep my mind on business. All, I think about is you. Your soft touch, your eyes telling me how much you want me. I wonder how much longer I can keep my promise." He kissed her, promising to show her how deep his passion ran. It was a long, breathtaking kiss.

When they exhausted the passion in the kiss, Kaine took a deep breath and confessed. "I admit I've wanted to kiss you like that for hours. You make me so happy knowing you're here. It's been so long since I've had a woman's tender love. I'm a dead man coming back to life."

She watched him add a magnetic smile she would follow anywhere.

"If you consent, I've arranged our third date. To stay here overnight. We would have Briarwood Castle all to ourselves. Then I can kiss you and love you whenever you want. I heard your wish for this spell we're in, to go on forever. The problem is — I don't have forever. I don't even have many hours. I don't live an ordinary life, so I can't court you the way I want because my world moves too fast.

"If I'd met you before this tour started, I would have taken my time, and given you the time you need. But fate was not kind. I have to look at the bright side. As untimely as our meeting is at the beginning of an eighteen-month world tour, we have found each other." Kaine explained, then stopped. He looked at her curiously, as his tongue licked his bottom lip and then tucked it under his top lip. His eyelids narrowed.

He was telling her, he's trapped, please understand. It had been the same dilemma with Luka. Duty or heart? Luka had found one way to give her a special morning. He had never been free of obligations after that long enough to ask her to stay the night, and, as a result lost her to Kaine. Now, Kaine would give her a second night. Their third date, and she knew what that meant.

Before her next thought, Kaine quickly continue.

"After tonight, I will have used up all the unscheduled time I have for proper dates. The next four days are in London. The schedule is overbooked with photo shoots, sound checks, interviews, a recording session, a concert, and a benefit. It never ends. Then I'm off to Paris, and the process begins again. I don't have much time I can give you each day. I can promise all of this night with you. I can stay, and I can give you all my attention until tomorrow. I promise you all of me you can handle."

Kaine sat quietly, a vision of a majestic, elegant, romantic time traveler waiting for an answer. His body tensed as he raised his chin like a nobleman. His eyes filled too fast with a twitch of doubt as if he didn't understand her hesitation.

She was mute, shocked, and in awe of his romantic invitation. She watched fear pushing his doubts away, thinking she would not stay. Holly prepared her answer. She had four days left of her seven-day contest winnings before she too had to return to L.A. After that, who knew what plan they would arrange? If this charismatic singer was asking her for one more night, then she wanted all of him, for as long as possible. She watched his eyes flicker, enticing her with long dark lashes that waited patiently for an answer to his future with her.

Holly smiled slowly at first.

Kaine squirmed within her embrace. He was groaning now,

as impatience captured his gaze that studied her as if trying to anticipate her answer.

Her smile grew broader as she imagined him kissing her with his kissable, sexy lips that begged her to kiss him again, again, and again. The whole idea of the castle and Kaine aroused a fountain of excitement. He must be able to see it on her face. How was she able to hide this blast of joy? She blurted out.

"Yes, oh yes. I'd love to spend the night here in this enchanted castle with you."

Kaine's face relaxed with immediate relief as his eyes flourished with delight. He flashed his darling bracketed dimples and then revealed the plan. "I have one last interview. By the time I'm finished, the crew will have cleared out. Then we will have the castle all to ourselves."

All to ourselves?

Holly repeated the dreamy words in her head.

Kaine's hand circled her waist and pulled her to the length of his body. She was riding a wild wave of pleasure, but she was also close to exhaustion. Holly wasn't sure she could continue with another fiery kiss. He must have sensed her resistance because he kissed her cheek and then let go of her, stood and whirled around to head in the direction of the control panel.

As an afterthought, Holly rose and gently caught hold of his forearm to stop him.

He shot her a piercing love-drenched look, that of a man who couldn't wait to get back to her.

Filled with a new confidence, coupled with her budding love, confessed under her breath, meant only for him, "I'd go anywhere with you."

Her words of trust seemed to bring him great pleasure. A gentle, sweet smile burst across his face more magnificent than any she'd previously seen. Again, his dimples charmed her to her toes.

"I'll be back as soon as I can," he promised. He kissed her quickly, a hot, branding kiss, telling her it wouldn't be long.

Holly scrounged for a deep, refreshing breath. She vowed in a quiet sexy tone.

"Tonight my Precious One, I promise we will do more than sleep."

Chapter Ten

YOU DON'T HAVE TO TELL ME

Holly's blissful mood was instantly shattered watching Luka return from barking orders to the crew that followed him.

"Come on mates, get this equipment packed up straightaway before the bleedin' gates of Hell open up and cuts us off from civilization. We need to get back to London straightaway before the nightlife begins without us."

Holly squirmed uncomfortably, chewing on the tips of her nails. Kaine was whispering into Luka's ear. She waited for Luka's explosive reaction to Kaine's news.

Luka did not disappoint.

His eyes blasting from his sockets told her she was right to be concerned. He shot a confused, heart-piercing look, straight across the room to Holly.

His one question clear.

Why?

His disillusionment is obvious.

Kaine was mid-sentence when Luka left him. He walked with purpose toward her, his piercing blue eyes condemning her, ordering her to change her mind, quickly.

The adrenaline pumped quickly into Holly's veins, moving at breakneck speed. Too much was happening, moving too fast. She faintly heard Kaine called away for the last interview. She dropped her head down, breaking Luka's unrelenting stare. She shifted her weight and hid her eyes by shutting them, searching for the courage to hold her ground, instead of running and hiding somewhere in the castle with Kaine. It would be so much easier, simply to run far away from Luka's disillusioned eyes that screamed — tell him it wasn't true. She steadied herself for the brunt of landfall. She hoped, the few words, she'd chosen to explain, would end his frustration.

Holly waited for Luka to blast her.

Nothing happened.

Holly snuck in a tiny breath and lifted her chin. A second later, she cautiously opened her eyes. In her continued amazement, she stared into Luka's beautiful blue eyes. They were wide, and clear, sparkling more with each step closer to her. The blue in his eyes had softened to the color of a beautiful, serene lake found only in the high mountains. His expression so quiet and tranquil, it shattered the power of the intense moment.

When he was inches from her, he had put away his wand — enchantment accomplished. When he was a breath away, he playfully winked at her. His long platinum hair shimmered under the backdrop of the recording studio track lighting, making him appear beguiling and angelic. Or, was that because he shined whenever he looked at her?

No matter why, every time she looked at him, he became more beautiful. She'd discover something new on his face, like a small freckle she hadn't noticed. How obedient the hairs of his perfectly arched eyebrows were. Or, how tiny lines curled around the edge of his lips whenever he smiled. Or, his glistening lips when he licked them with his passionate tongue, preparing to kiss her to madness. She was always in awe of his exquisite masculinity.

His heartbeat thundered strong against her cool exterior, melting her will. He was claiming her once again as her body moved with him as if it belonged to him alone. Lost in the whirling spell, Luka, took her arm and led her to a room behind the control booth.

She couldn't be alone with Luka.

Anything but that.

Kaine had been so clear. If anything happened, this time, she would not be innocent.

There is a limit.

She glanced around to find a storage vault filled with recording tapes. The hundreds of black reel canisters lined the shelves, and all the labels read *Hurrikaine*. That was the last thought of her surroundings, as Luka closed in and consumed her, smoldering like a slow fire burning the wax of a candle. And even though she was near exhaustion, to be alone with Luka, and deny her attraction was awful, if not impossible. Why was it whenever she was alone with him, she would lose complete control over her body? Why was she always compelled to be close to him? To touch him? It had never been this way with any man before meeting him.

What was it about Luka Hunter that instantly lit a thrilling eruption of pleasure, like a wild wind blowing a fire across dry wheat fields? What was it about Luka that consistently confused her with a delicious blend of joyous pleasure, and then bone-grinding terror, knowing what she was risking if Kaine caught them?

Lost in the stolen moments, his expression said he was equally as mystified by her.

She smiled sinfully, lusting for him with an expectant look, fully aware if there were no Kaine Walker, she would shamelessly throw herself into his arms. She'd surrender to her scorching, volcanic lust exploding inside her for him.

Mmmm, Luka.

As usual, the passion was surging in her veins, energizing her, setting her afire. She wished that things were different, set free to indulge herself and drop to her knees, and finally taste him. Luka, her Luka, a recurring fever, no prescription, no cure. And each relapse worse than the last.

She attempted to hold back her fiery emotions, concerned she'd succumb and lose the battle.

Luka watched her fighting with herself, and he seemed to enjoy her losing the battle.

Holly was sure her eyes told him her heart's yearning, and desire, to sink into his arms, into his kiss, into his lusty fervor. Absorbed by Luka's magic, Holly missed the disloyalty cross her eyes, unable to recall why it was she shouldn't reach out and touch him, kiss him, and enjoy his touch. Luka with his long heavenly-kissed hair, his sexy body dressed in soft flannel, brushed denim, and supple leather. Everything about Luka screamed he was one hundred percent man.

He flicked a long lock of hair behind his shoulder, cocked his head to the side boyishly, lifted his eyebrows, and spoke softly. "I rather fancy being the focus of your lusty dreams. I see you're showing me no mercy." His breath warm, as it rolled over his bottom lip, carrying the familiar scent of a man that adored her.

"None." She verified in a low tone, grasping a breath, fighting the impulse to run a fingertip across his bottom lip. She looked at the fine, golden, strands of Luka's hair caught in his collar and reached up to free them. She affectionately draped them over his tiny, perfectly shaped ear with a tiny gold earring. What was this hot rush, she always experienced with Luka? Was it Love? Was it Lust? Did it matter anymore?

Trapped in the burning web with Luka, she'd never be free, but what was worse, to never know if she wanted freedom from him. She curled a long thread of his hair around her finger as natural to her as breathing. "Luka..." She mouthed more than spoke.

Would it always be this way? A contest for her heart. Never able to choose between them because they were the sum total of her perfect man. Which part of her perfect man could she live without missing? When she was with Kaine, she would choose him forever and always. When with Luka, she chose him, wondering why there was ever any confusion. And each time she was with Luka Hunter she swore he would be the only man she belonged to heart, body, mind, and soul.

Now, her only wish was to slip her hands behind him. To pull his hips to hers, then lean back with him on the tiny table beneath her, and make passionate love to him, creating unforgettable memories. The lustful dream left her speculating if he would be a sweet lover or a dangerous lover. No doubt, Luka would be both. "Luka..." She managed to say.

Luka moved closer, and his hand roaming care freely about her body made her swoon. A fresh wave of his crisp scent stole her breath away. When he pressed his lips on top of hers, she spun with dizziness. His kiss was gentle and slow. There was no fight in this kiss. He was not trying to convince her to stay with him. His kiss said he was content, like a warm, gentle, summer breeze, only wanting to hold her, be close to her.

Holly sank into his kiss, letting Luka show her the way to bliss. She had lost the battle within herself. So, she followed the overwhelming urge to kiss him back with more primal feelings than she'd ever shown him. The hardness of his rib cage, pressed against hers, the shallow pant of his breath set the rhythm of the kiss. Luka was as lost in this mystery as she was.

Wherever this magical place was that Luka whisked her away to, she never wanted to leave. He was the only one to take her to the secret place, created by Luka, the magician. Everything, including the universe, was at his beck and call. Apparently, creation was ready to invent an entirely new world especially for them.

She surrendered every part of her limp body because he had sucked her life from it, rendering her lifeless, left to drape along his curves like fine silk. When he pulled away from her, he slipped in a deep breath. She smiled, already knowing his next words before he spoke.

"You know now. Do I need to say ... I wipe the memory of Kaine from your mind?"

How deeply she hated those words — true words.

His eyes were flashing triumphantly, almost gloating, as he slipped his leg between hers and then raised the leg to rest his foot on a small wooden box. "You believe I don't understand. Perhaps, it's *you* that doesn't."

What did that mean?

Before she responded, he dropped his lips onto hers, then slipped his hands down the sides of her body until his hands cupped her derrière and pulled her up against him, straddling his thigh, moving her hips up closer to his.

With an unspoken rhythm, she pressed his swelling awakening against her belly, kissing her, unlike no other kiss.

Then, as if the wind changed, Luka stopped sucking her life's breath from her. His apprehension caused him to lose his usual quiet reserve as he fought his past, then the present, and for a future with her.

Luka, she wanted to cry out. The hot stinging tears of frustration building in her eyes, dropping out the corners and down the sides of her cheeks.

Luka did not hurry but lingered, showing Holly his brave new feelings for her. Was she sorry she had ever given him hope? Made Luka believe in love again? Was Holly sorry she'd showed Luka how much she loved him? Yes, yes, a thousand times yes. Her tears flowed easily. She was more in love with him at that moment than she should be. Luka was overshadowing all her thoughts, her body speaking to him in a new language he was teaching her. Before she grabbed a breath, he stood straight, allowing her to slide down his leg ever so slowly, followed by a sensual burn where he intended.

Luka took steps, directing her backward until she bounced

off the cold castle wall. That didn't stop Luka as he kept coming for her. She relaxed. He wouldn't stop until he molded his body to her contours. For the life of her, she couldn't think of any reason to stop him. Whatever her argument was, it vanished. His skillful hands roamed her body freely, knowing exactly when and where to stop, linger, and then move on, commanding her to betray Kaine. He pressed close enough for her to count the tiny freckles that kissed the high ridges of his cheeks. When he stared straight into her eyes, she looked back at him with eyes that no longer committed a sinful crime by being so close to him.

Holly wondered what he was thinking behind his half-lowered eyelids. As if Luka read her thoughts, he smiled his sexy smile. He had decided to take her with him, coiling his arms around her, flattening her against his firm body. Was there any part of her that didn't tremble or swell? Why didn't she stop him? But, how did someone stop the sun from rising?

She accepted the truth — she would never be free of Luka Hunter. He meant to kiss her until the last of her breath until she agreed to be his. She closed her eyes, unable to understand how he managed to strip her of all her defenses and good judgment, whenever he touched her.

She opened her glazed eyes and sighed. Luka's face was so close, his eyes were closed. His long, tawny, lashes a crescent shape. His full succulent lips were kissing her first one way, then the other, again, and again, and again. She clung to like a rag doll in his arms. Surrender completed. Luka won. The objective of the war is forgotten.

He stopped kissing her, but it didn't matter, she was blind. As the seconds passed, a half measure of her poise returned.

Holly inhaled a deep breath of the air.

"Don't ... don't pull away." He cautioned. "Don't be afraid of what we feel for each other. Let it be. Let it grow. Trust me, come to me." He invited in quick intervals as if his request was the most natural thing in the world. His thumb came out of nowhere to touch her lips. He smiled and admitted. "I fancy your lips swollen from my kisses." Then his succulent mouth covered hers again.

The dream state washed over her once more, pulling her down, holding her down, and baptized her to Luka. No longer able to stand on her own two feet, she struggled to straighten her legs but he controlled her picking exactly when, and where to touch her, to bring her the ultimate pleasure.

Holly rested her small hands on his broad, sexy chest.

He broke away from her, and she watched him suck in his wet lips. She relaxed her forehead in her hands.

What to do?

He made no more moves to kiss her breath away. He allowed shallow panting and warm puffs of his breath. Her sweet Luka's breath, in and out, in and out. Luka's breath blew, growing steadier. She was sure she would go crazy from this madness of wanting him. She was an addict in need of another fix.

Never, never, get enough.

Luka spoke. His voice echoed from the hollow of his cheek.

He spoke words she'd wanted from him since she had met him. Three little words — but not now — not now!

"Stay with me." His invitation, simple and clear.

She needed to give him a simple and clear answer.

But Luka wasn't going to make it easy for her. He didn't want to her to say no. "Come with me. I'll show you the best London has to offer. Then at midnight, you can show me no mercy." He drew in a breath and rubbed his cheek, with the days' growth of beard next to her, branding her his alone.

"Luka...."

Nooo. She screamed in the vacant halls of her mind. Now, he was romancing her, asking her to go on a date with him, he was offering her this night, an incredible evening of romance. But why now? Especially after Kaine told him, they were staying here. Because Kaine beat him and took her as his girlfriend faster than Luka expected.

Luka tightened his embrace. "I'll take you anywhere you want. I have the CMT jet. There must be many sunsets in the world we can find."

His compound invitation crushed her, his words sweet, loving, and so afraid. Luka was fighting for her.

"Luka..." She offered as she tried to step to the side and place distance between them.

He moved into close the gap, so overpowering, and mesmerizing.

Holly wondered what the exact words were to tell him she was shutting the invisible door.

She had to leave.

She must go.

She belonged to another man.

She hadn't fooled him — he'd known.

"Bloody hell, I won't press for now. It's good you're staying with Kaine. You will bloody well find out I'm not a liar. We will never build a future with you always wondering 'what if.' I understand. Kaine's spun his web of charm and sorcery. Listen to me — be careful. His Grace is going to pull out all the stops tonight. He's aware of the fact, that with the tour unfolding, he won't have another chance alone with you.

"Beware, Babe. He has a long history of violence and destruction, concerning women, especially with his girlfriends. Like his name's sake the hurricane, he destroys the one that is closest to him. Don't let that be you." Luka warned and stopped, holding his words tightly in his mouth until his cheek twitched.

What was it in his eyes that he wasn't telling her? What was the fear for her, she saw growing in his eyes? He leaned against her and tenderly kissed the rim of her ear. She wished he would stop because she was helpless, too weak from his kisses to ask him to stop.

He skipped his moist lips along her neck and spoke between kisses. "I can smell him on you, and I bloody hate that. I'm not sure how long I will stand by and watch a lady I adore, left emotionally crippled, or worse, because of that sod."

Holly lurched in his arms, not knowing how to ease his torment. A sharp, cold, pain stabbed her. She shivered in spite of Luka locking her in his warm embrace. He had broken her heart with his confession of impending distress, brought on by her staying with Kaine. Hot tears welled up in her eyes again as she remembered being devastated by the rejection. Left by someone you dearly cared about — hell, say it, loved!

Luka's scabrous words swept over Holly, echoing, frightening her. She hoped his cryptic warning was not a premonition of darker things to come, provoked by his jealousy. She wrapped her arms as tightly around Luka's waist as possible and pressed her cheek to his chest. In an instant, he wrapped his arms around her, hugging her tightly like a creeping vine. She guessed he was enjoying his gut-wrenching punch into her private fairy tale world. He may as well have been a parasite, for he had sucked out all the pleasure, and fantasy Kaine had lavished on her.

Holly lifted her chin inches away from his succulent, full lips, acutely aware of her distance, as she brushed her forehead dangerously near his mouth. Then, as a tumultuous wind, everything changed, it was too late. She looked deeply into his fucking, blue eyes to-die-for, and the armor fell away. His love for her flashed brilliantly in his eyes as he stormed at her.

"Go! Have your night." His reserve broke, his feelings oozing as if from a deep gash on his perfect face, no longer able to hide his anguish over losing her. "Blast! Stay with the bastard if you must." He declared with the power of a thunderbolt as his pride swiftly came to his rescue. "Go. Your love is no bloody good to me this way. I can't live with you holding a lingering love for Kaine tainting your eyes. But, I'll be damned if I'll ever let you forget me."

Like a warhead, Luka's words tore deep into her heart of hearts as he simultaneously covered her mouth violently with his, crushing her.

She never thought to put up a fight.

His tongue entered powerfully, angrily. He was fuming and was going to make a point.

She welcomed him. Her hands magnetically slid up the soft, leather fabric of his jacket sleeves, over his muscles twisting underneath his skin. He moved his body with the rhythm she recognized, that of her sweet Luka, relaxing and kissed her oh, so lovingly. No, urgency. His tongue started to slow-dance, gently with hers. The sweet affection fused them to each other, consuming their bodies, then minds, and then their souls.

Luka's kiss was showing Holly the way back to the secret place. He added a gentle rocking of his body as his hard love took form, fighting for release. His breath was long, labored, and now matched hers.

Mmmm, Luka...

She held onto him accepting the way.

He revealed his need, a new, flourishing adoration, showing her all the joy he would bring her, living with him in the secret place. His kiss grew more insistent, seized with a new panic. He kissed her deeply, more devotedly as if almost afraid to let go of her for fear of what would happen to her if he allowed her to go with Kaine.

Holly kissed Luka until his panic faded. Until his body was relaxed, fitting about hers as the ancient vine around the castle, so natural, so right. He was changing her destiny, forming an invisible bond she wasn't sure anyone, especially Kaine, could ever break. But she hoped Luka would have enough strength for both of them, to walk away from her.

Seemed he didn't.

Holly kissed her beautiful golden angel with all the love she had denied him unable to stop the mournful tears that dripped quietly from the outer edges of her eyes. She filled with regret, so sorry, her love would not grow stronger for him every day for the rest of her life. Tears dropped. There would be no future, no long nights or mornings of loving each other. She wept over never having him full sized inside her, showing her all the mysteries of his lovemaking. She wept because they never had a chance to discover the hopes and dreams that weave a lifetime together.

This time was her last kiss — with him.

This time had to be a final goodbye.

Kaine was right about Luka and she reaffirmed her choice — she wanted Kaine.

Luka pulled away. He must have sensed her thoughts.

To look in his eyes brought condemnation. She hated herself for the sorrow she saw shadowing his eyes. There was no hint of condemnation, but the sparkle had unmistakably vanished, his eyes slightly red, glistening with tears he fought back.

She'd never of imagined this strong an emotional response from Luka.

She heard her heart shatter.

Or, was it his?

It was difficult to bear the intense ache, the dreadful guilt, and the sullen tone in his eyes. Holly looked away from her beautiful Luka — their parting — devastating.

Sadly, she leaned into his chest.

His arms grew tight about her shoulders, hugging her protectively, silently telling her he would always care for her.

The words she spoke were empty and echoed in his chest.

"This is not what I wanted. You maintain that you weren't hurting because you hadn't lost. You have the advantage, you know Kaine. So, I suppose this makes no sense. But...."

He lifted her chin with a curled finger, gazing deeply into

her eyes, and filled in the remainder of the sentence. "But? To erase any last doubts, your curiosity compels you to stay with Kaine?"

"It's not about curiosity. I've made a commitment to him and he has made one to me. We've agreed."

He laughed with disgust and scoffed. "You're saying after one night, you fancy Kaine. I thought you were a more sensible lady. You barely know him."

"I barely know you and look how I feel."

Checkmate!

Luka remained silent.

Holly lifted her hand and traced the line of his full lips with her nail tip.

"Will you be all right?" She quietly comforted.

"Do I look that bloody stupid?" He snapped, grabbing her hand.

"You're bloody asking me to send you into Kaine's arms with my blessing?"

She bristled.

"That's not quite what I meant," she assured. But, he was right. She wanted Luka to set her conscience free to love Kaine wholly, and exclusively.

"I'm not a fool." He rebuked.

"I won't make it easy — and I won't beg."

"Words can't change the feelings that have happened between Kaine and I. Feelings I didn't want," she half-blurted out, not knowing how to ease the situation.

"Thank you for looking out for me. But, I'll be all right," she added.

Luka's whole body grew rigid. He took her shoulders in his

powerful hands as if to shake her like an obstinate child to wake up before she made a big mistake.

He stared straight into her eyes again. His pupil's dark, raging with a jagged edge.

"I don't want your bloody thanks. I want you ... your — never bloody mind. I swore I wouldn't beg. Remember, you're never going to be out of harm's way with Kaine. Never...."

Chapter Eleven

WAITING FOR A GIRL LIKE YOU

L uka surrendered. The expression in his eyes reflected his unbearable heartbreak. They also echoed his fear for her safety. He draped a long lock of his luscious hair over his ear, turned, and walked out of the room. He never looked back.

Luka left Holly more bewildered if that was possible.

Lilly's words flashed through her mind.

Before anyone gets hurt.

Well, she'd done that. It was far too late for that advice. Someone had already been hurt. Luka, her angel-eyed Luka. She wanted to be happy, elated, on top of the world. She had Kaine to love for as long as he would have her.

Why was she miserable, unhappy, and torn apart?

Why did she hate herself?

"How could things get messed up so quickly?" She admonished, feeling cursed as she wiped away tears of frustration dripping from the corners of her eyes. There wasn't any time to detox herself from Luka's compelling words, his kisses, his scent, and the perfect feel of him. Where was she to put all of these shattered feelings before she met up with Kaine? Maybe there was a box marked 'falling in love with Luka' placed at the rear of a shelf in the dark corridor of her mind? And would these riotous feelings wait patiently for Kaine to set them free? Or, would they wait until Luka returned, spring alive, and drive her out of her mind? Because she knew, he would return.

Holly stormed out into the control booth.

A crewmember stood waiting for her and explained, "Kaine asked for you. He's out front."

Now, what?

It was time to get over Luka and fast. Kaine would not accept a second indiscretion. How the hell was she supposed to flip a switch and be ready and waiting for Kaine? This world was moving exceedingly fast. It had become impossible for her to continue to bounce between Kaine and Luka.

As she started her long journey to the outside of the castle, she thought to develop a plan. With every step she took, her heart grew more crestfallen. She was abandoning her golden angel, who had trusted and believed she would fall in love with him. She'd admitted she cared for Luka, perhaps too much. On the other hand, she not only cared for Kaine, but she'd committed to him.

Holly headed down a long, dark corridor inside the mysterious sanctuary. From out of nowhere, a hand snagged her around the waist. Before she could speak, the mysterious hand pulled her into a hidden alcove tucked away in the thick brick wall.

Kaine surrounded her the same time as the luscious scent of

his cologne. He engulfed her with his magnetic passion as only he could. Consumed by his urgent wish to kiss her, she clung to his shoulders. She pressed her lips hungrily against his, for fear, there may be a thread of truth to Luka's accusations.

They stood uninterrupted for a few seconds, meshed as one. Holly needed the time to acclimate herself — that these starry-eyed kisses belonged to Kaine. She found it hard to believe this kiss from Kaine, so steeped in warmth, could be the wrong choice, according to Luka, and be the kiss of a cold and cruel man. Enough — she'd made her final choice. She'd closed the door to Luka, leaving him deep in the secret place, looking forward to giving Kaine her complete attention.

Within seconds, Kaine accomplished the impossible. He'd replaced the taste of Luka with his, the feel of Luka's body with his, and her passion for Luka with a re-ignited fire for him sooner than she would have believed possible. Random thoughts of Luka's warnings faded, and then Luka himself became a faint memory, and then vanished.

When Holly came up for air, Kaine was devoted to her.

"What is it?" he asked his question in a cautious voice as if he sensed her dilemma.

"Nothing," she stated with a flat tone, hoping to avoid any more confrontations. She clung to Kaine, filling her thoughts with only him.

"Smashing. I have a surprise for you." He delivered the words into her hair and led Holly out of the fortress.

She glanced up at a slate gray sky, dotted with black threatening clouds. It was cool, and a pesky, brisk breeze kicked about the grounds. They walked hand in hand over the grassy knolls without saying a word as if one skin, one thought, and one breath. At the summit of the second knoll, Holly looked down onto a wondrous valley with a large, dilapidated, building that looked like at one time, was a grand mansion. To the left sat another huge T-shaped building, behind both of them a thick forest.

"What is that?" She queried as they continued to walk.

"That is Briarwood Manor and the building next to it are the stables," Kaine explained as he maneuvered down the knoll. They walked a bit, and he led her into the stables, and along the dozen or so horse stalls.

"If you're interested, we can hitch up a buggy? You game?" he asked, his eyes dancing with joy like a kid before opening his birthday presents.

"Dressed like this? We'll freeze." Then the thought disappeared as she admired Kaine. How regal and noble he stood in his black velvet cloak that hung with long slender folds. He held his carriage tall and commanding as a prince.

"You said you wanted a fairy tale fantasy? Well, how much closer can we get? I have warm coats, and thick blankets to keep us warm. Are you game, My Lady?" His eyes pleaded for her to continue pretending as he produced two wool-lined Mackintoshes.

How could she tell him she was physically and emotionally exhausted? That she longed for a hot bath, and then a long, refreshing nap, or how her back ached, and her bottom was sore from riding a horse all afternoon?

She surrendered.

"Of course, I'm ready, My Lord." Then enthusiastically slipped her fingers between Kaine's, and with the other, grabbed her gown at mid-length.

She pulled him along in front of the musty stalls, searching for the right horse.

"Finally," she announced to Kaine as she stopped in front of a magnificent, ebony stallion aptly named Wicked. Exactly how she felt, she mused.

"He's my favorite too," Kaine, agreed, flashing his dimples. Then returned to work with Wicked, who seemed to know him.

The casual act prompted Holly to ask, "How do you know Wicked? You know the owner?"

Kaine fussed with the bridle of the shiny black stallion.

"Sometimes I think I do. Other times? I don't. He travels a lot, quite moody. A loner of sorts." He commented while adjusting the bridle.

"With a grand estate like this, why would he ever leave?"

"Forced to keep up his investments."

"Do you have any idea why a man who seems to have everything would allow the castle to remain in such disrepair?"

"From what I understand, he gave up trying. No passion in his life, no need to build."

"No woman you mean? Well, I can understand that. I wouldn't want a man that would give up either. I want a man like you that will fight."

Kaine stopped as if listening intently to her words. A serious look pushed his eyebrows together.

She noticed he went to a mysterious place where his thoughts held him captive. She knew he wasn't aware she had read the private requests on his desk back at the hotel. He wasn't the kind of man who would want her to know what a real champion of the people he was. She raised a curious brow. What could be bothering him?

Kaine's face grew pensive. He started to speak but stopped to prepare Wicked. He had trouble because the spirited stallion was clearly more horse than the buggy required. After calming the spooked horse, Kaine spoke, and he couldn't have surprised her more.

"What if … your work was not an anchor, but a way to become free? What if … your work stripped away the outer perimeters and all conventional boundaries, associated with ordinary life? What if … to become yourself, there were few limits imposed? And to burst through any of these remaining limits dreamed of, were rewarded with money? More money than you ever thought possible. Now, there are no limits left. You have enough money to break, or manipulate any laws because men make laws, and engage solicitors, barristers, and judges, who can be bought to find holes in the laws."

Holly was blown away by his philosophical questions and provocative speech. She leaned against the carriage in awe, but mostly concern. He certainly was an outlaw of his times. She'd listened to him describe a world that sounded horrible. No laws, no rules, no guidelines? Her whole world consisted of making round things fit squares. Then Kaine interrupted her internal evaluation of his speech.

"Assume this fighter has climbed to the top of his profession and found out that nothing is there. He learns too late that it's empty at the top. Lifeless. The whole idea of happiness is friends, family, and relationships, combined with the struggle to get to the top. He is left disillusioned by life and exhausted," he explained, seeming a little embarrassed by his outburst, and quickly returned his focus to working on the bridle.

Wicked was not happy, flicking his tail and kicking outwardly with his rear hoof. Kaine tried to calm him by stroking his dark muzzle.

"Was all that about the man that owns Briarwood? Or, have you added a bit of your own personal philosophy?"

Kaine didn't look at her but remarked, "It's a subject I've had long discussions with him. What to do when you're thirty-two and have achieved all your dreams, and beyond your imagination?"

"There's nothing to discuss. There is a simple answer."

"Simple? And what, pray tell Miss Hill is the answer?"

"Please, don't make fun of me. I'm not Pollyanna, but I believe you create new dreams, Kaine. There is so much good to be made in the world. A rich, selfish person as the man that owns Briarwood, what does he do to help the others that suffer?"

She thought about the thick stack of request that Kaine had written — *Give them what they want. Don't sign my name.*

"Well, I pity him. He will probably die a lonely man."

"If he hasn't died already."

"What do you mean died?"

"I mean, sometimes loneliness can kill you when you're alive. It takes a bit longer."

How morbid. But Kaine's words of truth moved her heart. She realized some of what he had said was about himself, yet — why was he alone? He was alarmingly gorgeous, wealthy, smart, and so talented. Why had Kaine Walker, imposed on himself a four-year retreat from life?

Kaine straightened up, shook his hair about his shoulders, and declared. "Enough philosophy. Let's get going. You can help me spin new dreams."

"You were talking about yourself," she confirmed.

"Some. That comes as no surprise to an intelligent lady like you."

They climbed into the centuries old buggy, and Kaine took hold of the reins and expertly guided a spirited Wicked out of the stables. They trotted along the ribbon of the road that etched a pathway over the impressive knolls. They passed the ivy-covered castle, then the last of the crew.

Holly sat with her fairy tale, fantasy, rock-star, prince, shaking her head in unbelief. Soon the crew looked like a child's toys, scattered about, puny and unimportant. After some time, Kaine halted at the summit of a high ridge.

The incredible panoramic view and a patchwork of the enchanted valley rendered Holly awestruck. In the far corner, sat a child-sized village with a dark, uninviting forest stretching its arms to the horizon.

"Oh, Kaine. It is truly breathtaking. What is that?"

"Dunnehill Village, named after the castle."

"I thought this was Briarwood Castle?"

"Been renamed."

"You know a lot about this area?"

"I spent a lot of time in the Dunnehill pubs. I come from this part of the country. I assure you what I know is common knowledge."

"What a beautiful place to call home."

Kaine didn't answer. He was lost again in his mysterious

thoughts. She'd notice he would often fall into lapses of contemplation, leaving her to speculate on what attracted his attention. Were the memories that occupied his thoughts happy ones? Or, did his demons, and shadows play with him, tormenting him?

Holly gazed long and hard at Briarwood Castle as if mesmerized. It stood tall, commanding, rising up to respectfully kiss the hem of the darkening gray sky. The clouds lurked about the top of the turrets like a dark crown, threatening and imposing. A colder, brisker wind kicked up and it was icy and relentless, splashing two red spots on Kaine's cheeks from the lashing winds.

She remembered his back. How horrible the memory was — those vile lashes. She slid over, ran her hand up to his shoulder, molding herself into the crevices of his body as if created only for him and hugged him fiercely. He needed so much love, real love — true love, and she hoped hers would be enough.

Kaine quickly responded, wrapped his arms around her and then brought his hands up to creep deep into her hair, holding her head. He searched her eyes as he cradled her. "Where does this tenderness come from, My Lady?" His tone is soft and sweet.

"I don't know." She lied. "I'm so glad you don't own this estate. You would do so much good." She speculated with confidence. She hugged him again and kissed his cheek now covered with a day's growth of beard.

"I like it better when your eyes shine with joy," he admitted a breath away from her mouth.

"I do feel happy, incredibly happy," Holly confessed. She

snuggled into Kaine's familiar arms.

The cold, cruel wind was stabbing like needles into the flesh of her face, but she didn't mind, she had Kaine to keep her warm. "What's that?" she finally remembered to ask.

"Briarwood Cottage, and beyond where the stream empties into the pond, the boat house."

"Are you telling me all of this land is Briarwood?"

"Yes, Briarwood is as far as you can see."

"Excellent. This estate would be a magnificent place to live." She realized too late, what she had blurted out, and she couldn't take back the words.

Kaine gently laughed. "I see. You have already changed your mind if you were the owner of Briarwood."

"Briarwood mine? I doubt the owner and I could ever get along, Kaine. Don't get me wrong. I would love to live here with the right man." The last two words she spoke low.

"You wouldn't want to live here alone?"

"No."

"Why?"

"Too big, I would get lonesome. I suppose I could get involved in putting the estate to work. An estate this grand would generate vast sums of money to be put to good use. Maybe, help political prisoners or help make reforms. Maybe, for environmental causes, terminally ill people, for defending people unfairly accused of horrendous crimes they didn't commit. The list is endless."

Holly sat in a dream state thinking of all the good she could do as the Lady of Briarwood. But that dream was beyond all possibilities.

Kaine clicked his tongue in his mouth, and Wicked

followed the worn trail. "Is that why you work as a clerk for a solicitor, to see justice done?"

His words caught her off guard.

She gathered her thoughts and proceeded. "No, nothing so altruistic, though I'm ashamed to say, I'm not much different from the man that owns Briarwood. It seems right that Briarwood has shown me that I too have been selfish, hiding from the world. I've been too irresponsible to see I need to take the bar exam, get my license, and practice law on my own. What would you think of that?" What she didn't say was, she'd finally get out from under Brett's thumb.

"You want to become a solicitor? Change the rules?"

"I am a solicitor, I mean attorney ... except for the license. To set the record straight, I don't have any interest in trying to change the rules. I want to enforce the existing rules. I practically tried the last case I worked on, only Brett...." She barely had time to finish because Kaine cut her off to speak.

"Who is this Brett?" He quickly questioned as a dark shadow settled over his handsome, pale features. Oh, those Technicolor blue eyes, dreamy eyes, that would look deep into her soul and then look past her like through a pane of glass.

Holly spoke out too quickly, "He's a criminal attorney I work with in L.A., and he's expecting to become my husband when I return." She'd fought to control her voice pitch starting high and positive and then dropping on the word husband. How ridiculous that word sounded. She had no more intentions of marrying Brett than to sprout wings and fly from that very spot.

Kaine jerked Wicked to stop. His face turned toward her. His expression testified that he couldn't be more astonished.

Then he smiled one of his incredible, warm smiles showing his bright, shiny, white teeth. He laughed loudly and admitted in a tone of great awe.

"Your husband! You're fucking engaged to be married while all of England believes you to be my secret girlfriend? Who I might point out *is* my girlfriend, and about to spend the night in an enchanted castle alone with me? Miss Hill? How many more dark secrets do you have?"

Holly elbowed Kaine in his ribs for teasing her unmercifully. But she loved feeling she belonged when he referred to her as his girlfriend, and it had been too long since she belonged anywhere.

He continued to laugh, even more dramatically.

She bristled a bit. It wasn't that funny. "Of course, I no longer have any intentions of marrying him. But now, on second thought, maybe I should marry Brett. He doesn't laugh at me." She sassed back at Kaine.

His face went ashen. "No," he snapped.

"No, what Kaine?"

"No, don't marry Brett." His voice seemed tight, distraught, as his laughter drained with the reality that she was promised to another. He quickly lifted her left hand to investigate. "You're not wearing a ring?"

She decided to stop paying him back for hurting her feelings.

"I have no intentions of marrying Brett. The ring is at home in my bedstand drawer. I have to find a gentle way to tell him I can't marry him."

Kaine looked at her. His color had returned to his face before he probed. "It's not often I can be surprised. But you,

My Lady Love, are a woman filled with delightful surprises. Tell me, Holly, truthfully. Would you marry a man you did not love?"

She was too ashamed to say she almost had. Instead, she answered, "Never."

Kaine sat back, visibly relieved, and encouraged Wicked to begin walking again.

She stole a glance at him out of the corner of her eye. Kaine Walker was the kind of man that one could never take their eyes off because he was terminally handsome in hundreds of ways. Holly had plans to count each of them every day for the rest of her life.

She placed her attention on the road straight ahead and aired her thoughts in a low voice.

"I have to find a way to tell Brett."

The words floated into the silence.

They rode deeper into the vast estate of Briarwood.

Minutes passed.

"I think I can help you. That is if you'd allow my help," Kaine said.

"You?"

"A gentleman to the rescue and all that rot." Kaine maintained, gallantly bending at his waist dismissing her comment.

Something else was weighing on his mind.

He stopped Wicked again. This time, he stepped out of the carriage, circling around to her side and offered his hand, palm up for her to take. As she stepped out, he urgently swept her into his strong arms. Another long, impassioned, lingering kiss left Holly faint and disoriented.

"Holly." Kaine paused as if measuring each word, his breath a cloudy mist of warm air. "I have to tell you." Then he shared more insistent. "I wanted to save this for the right moment. After your bombshell, I think it's arrived. I may have one of my own, and hopefully the solution to your problem."

Holly held her breath. What could Kaine possibly do to help her tenuous situation with Brett? More importantly, was she strong enough to hear it.

"This is going to sound ridiculous coming from me ... ah, well, let's say a chap in my line of work. But you, My Lady, have brought out my best behavior. I'm not usually like this. In fact, I've never been this way. But Holly, I woke up this morning, glad to be alive because you, My Lady Love, were lying beside me. I thank destiny because you're a wondrous gift."

Kaine paused again, and a little insecurity lined his eyes. He drew in a deep breath, bolstering his confidence. He ran the tip of his tongue across his bottom lip. The sheen on his lips glowed like a light beacon sending loving signals into the dark, stormy sea of her sentiment.

Kaine looked up to gaze at the stormy sky.

She joined him noticing the threatening sky was dense with coal-black, menacing, clouds shaped like a black mask, concealing any hint of the moon or stars.

He spoke again. Each word measured in a husky tone.

"I've waited so long for you." He looked back down to her and pulled her into his strong embrace.

He held her up as she waited for more of his words. She floated, hearing only the pounding of her heart, and evidently, her legs had given out because she couldn't stand.

Kaine nudged his cold nose into her hair nuzzling her ear and explained. "Anyone around me seen me go off the deep end a few times. This time, I want to go slow. I want to prove to everyone, but mostly to you, that I've never felt this way, that this wonderful feeling is real. I'm afraid to call it love, especially since it happened so fast. I've been disappointed when I've used that word in the past to describe my actions.

"But I want you to know that I am solid, that this wondrous feeling is real, not part of the fantasy of the castle." He held her tight for a bit and then dropped his head back. His foot long hair touched the place where his belt would be. Kaine straightened his head and ran his fingers through the front of his hair, fanning it about his shoulders like a dark cloak.

"I've purposely been alone for years because I've been so disillusioned when it came to committed relationships with women. These feelings I have for you are incredibly new to me. Please, believe me. They're not like any other time."

Kaine seemed to become more elated with his revelation, picking up momentum with each word.

"My Lady, I will do this right." And as if forced by a magic spell, Kaine fell onto one bent knee.

She hoped to remain standing, for he had swept her off her feet with his words of love — a poet's words.

Kaine Walker, rock star prince, held her hand gently like a delicate snowflake. He pressed his cool mouth to her hand, brushing it with his soft lips ever so lightly. His beautiful, Technicolor blue eyes looked up at her filled with emotions as sweet as honey.

A moment later, the dream man confessed.

Chapter Twelve

DREAM UNTIL TOMORROW

Kaine Walker whispered, "I want you to know … I'm already in love with you, My Lady."

The words were magical with the smooth, melodic voice of a seraph. His sweet face shined brightly with his new feelings for her, and his radiant smile showed off his darling dimples.

All the while, Holly Hill stood reveling in his words, barely exhaling a solitary breath. His words floated into her head and then into her heart, like dream smoke filtering into secret places never touched by another man.

Kaine stood up straight and tall beside her. She gazed up into the crystal, blue, labyrinth of his eyes. There she found his love stretching into an endless void. Her grateful tears spilled, trickling down her cheeks while her magnificent Kaine read her reaction with joy.

"I've loved you since our first kiss," she humbly managed in a soft voice.

Kaine's face stretched with the brightest smile she'd ever seen. He wrapped his arms around her and lifted her high into the air, euphorically twirling her around in a circle. Kaine let her slip slowly down the front of him.

As her lips reached his face, she lavished him with her wet kisses. She stopped at his perfect heart shaped lips. Holly pressed softly at first, and then more insistent, telling Kaine, she would love him all the moments of time.

Between successions of kisses, he admitted. "I believe I knew backstage, in the darkness, the first night at the concert. I never wanted to leave you then … all I wanted to do was kiss you forever."

"You know I do see you."

"Yes, my lovely lady. You see *me*."

Kaine led Wicked by the reins. He seemed too full of joyous energy to ride in the carriage as he followed the path heading toward the stables.

Holly strolled with her charming prince arm-in-arm. They walked down the grassy knoll laced with sprigs of brightly colored, fragrant flowers mysteriously wrapped in the swirling mist.

"Well, I guess it's important I ask you formally, without the press forcing our hand. I'm going to ask you to be my special, and only lady since you weren't given much choice. How does that sound? Kaine Walker — yours forever?"

"It sounds perfect, and yes, My Lord, I would be, so proud to become your forever lady."

She felt his smile.

The sleepy English sun peeked out to christen their magical union and then had quickly slipped between the scattered black and gray clouds that foretold of a record-breaking storm. The night temperature had dropped rapidly bringing a frosty chill.

The long, cricketed shadow of the castle started to creep, draping itself across the land beneath it like a giant velvet blanket filled with many dark secrets. They passed exquisite gardens and at last, arrived at the stables. In the seconds that passed, their new world became a sheath of darkness. Kaine lit a lantern and lost somewhere between falling in love and being in love, the fairy tale lovers worked together to groom and feed Wicked.

It was a soothing interlude to help Holly regain her balance. She needed to focus on something other than her fiery attraction to him.

They strolled hand-in-hand to Briarwood Castle towering above them harshly and imposing. A cool mist danced around the ground like imps and devils preparing for a sacrifice. The castle was astonishingly daunting in the evening's twilight, frightening, and overpowering like in a child's distorted nightmare. The square turrets rose higher than she'd remembered. Her limited vision could not take in the full sight of the stronghold all at once. It soared three times the height of the surrounding trees. A hypnotic stillness shrouded the castle setting off her internal warning system.

Kaine led Holly, tramping midst another beautiful, but smaller garden. The flowers alongside her feet were becoming deep shadows that sparkled in the mist. She shivered, unexpectedly wanting to flee this place, and return to London. She didn't want to enter the keep. It seemed as if a giant might have passed under the archway and awaited her return. The thick stonewall mocked her, refusing to reveal the layers thick with secrets, hundreds of years of dark secrets. Moreover, she heard the mild hum of whispers from the past warning her.

Everything about the castle frightened her, especially the black shadows, empty windows, and thick, lead, stained-glass windows. The top of the walls crenelated battlements, and the shadowed alcoves, provided a perfect place for more evil spirits, and fiends to hide. Even the buttress that supported the external walls of the chapel appeared suffocated with malevolence.

Why had she agreed to stay with Kaine here?

Holly clung to Kaine.

"What is it Holly?" he asked with concern.

"I don't like the castle in the dark, let's not stay." A gust of icy wind stole the last of Holly's warmth away. She shrank from the bitter cold, pulling the coat tighter convinced she'd never been this cold. The surroundings went black in the blink-of-a-eye, and she lost all sense of direction while her intuition screamed danger.

Kaine slowed his pace so she would not stumble over the chipped and broken cobblestones.

She barely saw him glance over his shoulder.

He encouraged her, "Let me give you a fairy tale fantasy. Let me love you here, please, stay here with me Holly. When we return to London, we will seldom be alone. There's always someone within calling distance, be it assistants, the media, fans, not to mention security. Here, to be with you entirely alone tonight is a great privilege and pleasure for me.

"Try to understand why I don't want to leave. Call me selfish, spoiled, or sensible. It's going to storm soon. For practical reasons, you and I cannot be on the motorbike heading for London when the storm strikes. On the other hand, don't allow the castle's dark charm scare you. You're with me — trust me — relax and let the castle's enchantment work its magic."

"That's easy for you to say. You face tens of thousands of people. You're not afraid of anything."

"Your words are kind. I wish I were as brave as you believe. That might have been true a few days ago, but now, not so true. After my recent declaration, I am afraid of losing you."

Holly squeezed Kaine's hand meaningfully, knocked entirely off guard with his directness. This man unequivocally disarmed her in seconds with a few well-chosen words. She wanted to say something equally grand to Kaine but didn't have the words.

The walkway was pitch black, and she grew more nervous with each second. Holly dragged her fingertips along the jagged surface of the wall to calm her escalating fears as Kaine guided her inside the keep like a blind woman.

They entered the medieval entrance. Kaine struck a match from an antique holder. A sconce appeared on the wall, and he lit the wick. The light shed a broad bar of golden light down a long, vast corridor. Kaine walked quickly as his footfall clicked on the stone floor and flicked a switch, lighting another row of electric wall sconces resembling Old World candelabras.

The lights brought a bit of temporary relief, and protection as the inner glamor of the castle brought her to her knees. The simple elegance and raw masculine beauty, of a real English castle, were astounding. "Why hasn't the owner restored this castle to its former splendor, and glory? This magnificent piece of the old world could be a showplace." She claimed in an amazed tone.

"Perhaps he wishes it to be a home. Not a place for stupid tourists to come and tramp about day after day."

She sensed an unsettling gloom caught in Kaine's voice as she glided along the edges of his cool tone. How mysterious he was, she never expected anything he said.

Kaine walked with long, grand strides, and the sounds of his boot heels were clicking a different sound because the flooring had changed to century's old, polished wide-plank wood.

She followed the echoes of his footsteps as he pushed open two beautifully scrolled doors. Holly was even more captivated as she whirled about in a circle on her toes.

He explained, "Only the east wing has been restored to its original style, and splendor. It is complete with hidden upgrades. After that, the owner lost interest. That is where I planned we would stay, in a guest apartment. I hope this meets with your approval, My Lady?"

"Yes, wherever you decide." She agreed, hoping to gain a stronger sense of safety.

Kaine stopped and with a grand gesture pushed apart the doors. "This is the Great Hall."

Holly followed Kaine into the warmth of the exquisite dining room that looked like a lavish movie set, and lamented. "It's such a pity ... the castle could be, so beautiful."

"*IS* ... beautiful...." He corrected almost in a whisper.

A large candelabra stood lit, at the end of the grand table.

There an obligatory silver tea set sat with bone china cups and saucers. The elegant table set for two, on a white, embroidered cloth appeared impeccable. It ran horizontal topped with a gold accent runner and two place settings on each side. Displayed as pieces of art, the tableware was white, scalloped and accented with twenty-four karat gold. Next to each setting lay a beautiful, folded white-lace-edged napkin, topped with gold plated flatware, and above was crystal stemware.

The table was set perfect enough for Buckingham Palace. Along the wall, in the center of the room, awaiting their pleasure was a strong, crackling fire, growing fierce in the hearth. So mammoth was the carved, wooden mantel, it rose high above Kaine's head. The oversized mouth of the hearth reminded her of Monstro, the whale, in the story "Pinocchio," when his mouth had opened to swallow the puppet.

The eight centuries old fireplace invited her to come close, get warm, stay the night. In front, on a smooth, polished wood-planked floor was a twenty-by-twenty red rug. Centered on it, a thick, crème-colored Flokati shaggy rug, with large, inviting pillows strewn about it. She hurried over to the tempting hearth and turned her palms toward the fire to warm them. "Who did this?" She inquired.

"Part of the arrangements to stay. We have clothes. There is food warming in the kitchen. I'm sure I've thought of everything."

He definitely had. Holly wanted to run into Kaine's arms and thank him. However, something stronger than her impulsiveness held her back. It was something in the castle.

Somewhere, he had dropped off his noble cloak, and she watched as he raised his arm. The white, gauze, sleeve blew gently from a draft wrestling in the hearth as he rested his hand against the old wood-paneled wall. Kaine appeared almost supernatural, dressed in his romantic traveler costume. The glow from the logs flickered on his majestic face. He looked like he had always been here, belonged here, surrounded by all the antique tapestries and heavy drapes hanging about the high arched windows and walls. That's when she realized, she was *the* intruder. The time traveler sent back, stumbling on to him, here, hidden away from the world.

Kaine leaned beside the scrolled mantel. The soft, gauze-shirt hung loose edging his neck, begging her to come, and stroke the flesh of him. The magical trance was spun. The Lord of Briarwood Castle was at home with his Lady.

"Kaine," she asked in a cautious tone, daring to jar him from his mysterious contemplations.

"Yes, My Lady? I will take care of all your needs in good time." He assured as he quickly kneeled, and added another huge log to feed the hungry flames.

"I don't want any promises tonight," she pleaded in a low, even tone.

"I have one promise left, My Lady, to present you with a night you'll never forget. And perhaps together we will find forever love." He turned away from the hearth and walked closer to her.

Forever love.

The words had repeated in her mind before she spoke.

"Kaine you know exactly what to say. I can't match, or come close to your poet's words. So, please let me show you how I feel." She placed her hands delicately on his chest.

Kaine stiffened, and his expression cooled.

"Brett must have other ideas?"

"Brett? Why would you mention Brett?"

"He *is* your fiancé? You have shown him your love?"

"I've never loved Brett. It's been a given I'd eventually become a Brett's wife since college though we've never been intimate. I guess I've always accepted Brett would wait until our wedding night."

"You said you would never marry a man you did not love. How is it that you've entertained his proposal? More importantly, why would Brett show more restraint and gallantry than I?"

He paused, "Or, is it he's a bloody fool?"

She dismissed the complicated answer to why she would contradict herself and marry a man she didn't love. She decided to try to minimize her response.

"Neither. It's very complicated. I don't want to spend our evening talking about Brett."

Kaine wouldn't have it and continued to persist.

"Do you believe I am not gallant enough to wait for the wedding night with you?"

Wedding night?

Kaine was doing it again, throwing words at her, she couldn't possibly have imagined him saying. She had no idea how to process them, or to respond.

"It would seem that you can wait judging by your previous restraint," she managed to say.

Kaine pulled back, allowing a playful gust of wind to squeeze between them and in an agreeable tone conceded.

"I can be persuaded to wait. Our first night together can be as special as you want."

I can be persuaded. Wait!

He would wait because he wanted to make her happy. He was thinking in the future tense and giving her the choice of how their love would proceed. She'd never encountered anyone able to make her feel so incredibly special. Here stood this magnificent man asking her something she didn't understand.

As she closed the distance between them, she wondered if there was a marriage proposal somewhere in those powerful words.

"No wedding night will be sweeter than spending tonight in this enchanted castle with you, my Precious One."

"Are you saying you don't want to wait?" His eyes seemed guarded, almost disappointed.

There it was again. What was he asking? That she would not wait for their wedding night. Was this the enchantment of the castle doing what it did best, spinning fantastic fairy tales?

She didn't know how to proceed, so she offered. "I'm saying I want to treasure these special moments in this incredible fairy tale castle with you. Forever savoring each exquisite word you've spoken to a sacred place in my heart."

"You, my lovely lady will certainly drive me crazy with your sweet sentiments."

"There will never be another night as special as this one with you, my Precious One." She pointed out before she tiptoed up and kissed him once lightly on the lips though she wanted to kiss him again, and again.

He searched her eyes and then confessed. "I appreciate how you call me Precious One. It makes me special, as if one of a kind, maybe, extra special to you. I'm not sure if a woman's word has ever made me feel this way. You, My Lady, have your own special elixir of love." He dropped his sweet lips to brush hers. His tongue dipped in searching, deeper, and deeper, and then he stopped and admitted.

"You're such a mystery to me. I've never met a woman like you, Miss Holly Hill. So few women I knew came with a last bloody name. Of all the tens of thousands of women who claim to love me, there isn't one who would have refused my marriage proposal. Here I ask you, and I am refused. It seems, for now, I will have to be content with the moniker boyfriend, and not a husband."

Holly listened to his words riding on a breath into her heart. She was close to fainting, repeating those words in her mind.

Husband? When did Kaine ask to marry her?

In that shocking second, she realized she had turned down Kaine's marriage proposal. He was moving too fast. She did want the sanctity of his commitment, but she couldn't bring herself to say yes to marriage with a man she'd recently met, especially a dream man. She attempted to explain in hopes of putting him at ease.

"I want a man I marry to be passionately in love with me, not caught up in the enchantment. What if we wait until we are sure we are in love, and not under a lustful magical spell? If then you ask me again, I will marry you, Kaine, nothing will stop me," she stipulated enthusiastically.

Kaine seemed lost in another one of his mysterious thoughts. His words, so shocking tumbled from his lips. "So, let me understand. You believe that I don't know my own mind. My own heart? Or, the difference between love and lust? If I am so, befuddled, why would I ask you to marry me a second time? Or, is it … you? Does your rejection have anything to do with Luka?"

"Luka?" She blurted out as if struck by lightning.

Luka had been, so far from her thoughts. And, rejection? Every time she opened her mouth, she saw she was digging herself in a little deeper. Kaine decided she didn't want him, and she was holding out for Luka. What had she done? "Kaine, don't presume those horrible words you spoke are true because I do not have your flare with words. Never, would I reject you. Luka has nothing to do with you, and I. Look around, I am here tonight with you because somehow a miracle happened. I found you too. I do Kaine. I do. I found you to love, and to have, and to hold, until death us do part."

Kaine leaned forward with a forced smile, but something new stood between them.

What was it?

Kaine's tone remained guarded and as if unsure of her answer.

"So, you have, My Love. Let's soak in a hot bath. We will have a little to drink and a little to eat. Then My Lady Love, with your permission, of course, I shall ravish you until the sun rises."

She was relieved. She hadn't shattered their magical connection with her thoughtlessness.

His eyes had twinkled seconds before he kissed her madly.

When he pulled away, Holly realized how little she knew of this man to be so dazzled by him. Inside a relatively short period of time, they had betrothed themselves to each other with the possibility of marriage. All before, she had the knowledge of knowing how sublime to be mystically one with her.

How bewitched was he that he'd wanted her so quickly after everywhere he had been, and all the women. Oh, she couldn't think about them right now. How did he decide without ever making love to her, that she should become his wife?

Was it an enchantment?

Was anything real?

Or, was it only to be a night filled with dreams and illusions?

Kaine weaned her from his embrace and wove his smooth fingers into hers. He tugged at her hand, encouraging her to follow him to the foot of a long winding staircase, with a polished, scrolled banister. He stepped up on the first, marble stair, partially covered with red carpet, with frayed edges.

He mysteriously looked down into her eyes as if to search her soul, and then asked, "Are you ready?"

She smiled quickly and with an open heart confessed.

"I've waited my entire life for you."

Chapter Thirteen

LADY

Holly's thoughts spun like a carousel. She was convinced that when he shut the bedroom door, there would never be anyone like Kaine Walker in her life again. Soon she would find the missing part of her that had always held her hostage.

Kaine's magnificent face lit up brightly. He took another step tugging on her hand.

With each shadowy curve of the spiral staircase, Holly gave free reign to her deepest fears and doubts, opening the door of her private hideaway allowing them to shoot to the surface. With a giant breath, she let them all go. The new freedom was exhilarating.

With each step, Holly wanted to drop pieces of her costume on the dark winding staircase. She realized what a miracle it was to find a sensitive man that gave her his precious gift of time he didn't have, to become familiar with him. He'd offered assurance, even the sacred bond of marriage if she'd needed it. She was ready to become a whole woman, Kaine

Walker's woman, tonight, in this majestic setting befitting a queen.

They arrived at the third landing. Holly followed Kaine into a large, dimly lit room. Off to one corner was the spa area, glowing from a legion of candles. She was ready. Her mind filled with romance, her heart with love, her body with desire and her soul with joy.

The room was gigantic. It could easily hold her entire house in the canyon, including the yard. She thought to where she lived in a cozy, three-room cottage in Laurel Canyon, a neighborhood high in the hills above the Sunset Strip, in West Hollywood. As much as she loved the quaintness of her hide-a-way, this was a step back in time when the wealthy could afford such an enormous suite.

Kaine checked the heat setting on the thermostat and then walked over to the prepared bath in a mammoth, black-marbled tub in the corner of the room. It had a thick lip, perfect for the rows of candles. He generously poured purple oil into the sunken tub, and the room became scented with billows of lavender.

She followed him to the spa area and sat down on the lip of the whirlpool tub. She watched his every move as if bewitched, especially when she gazed into his beautiful, shimmering eyes whenever he glanced up at her. Eyes that said they adored her without the benefit of marriage.

Butterflies fluttered in her stomach, being so close to Kaine. Closer to him than any marriage paper could bind her than any church vow could unite her, believing wholeheartedly that even death could not separate her love for him.

Holly slid along the edge of the tub, helping him light the wick, one-by-one, slipping between the shadows cast by the scores of candles that lined the wide marble lip of the tub. Her head spun with one doubt, would she disappoint him? She was nervous as a maiden though she wasn't. She had belonged to another man, seven long years ago. But he had been a young, inexperienced man, learning the ways of loving. Not a world traveler, filled with the exotic experiences of a rock star. And tonight Kaine would make her forget him, no more painful memories, only Kaine.

He twisted the tap on slow to allow more water to fill the tub. He lit another long row of candles that lingered along the back of the thick ledge until it resembled pipes on a calliope. Then he pulled a John Roberts Blues CD, out of the black leather satchel, popped it into a hidden space in the wall, enhancing the ambiance of the soothing mood.

She kicked off her white, satin slippers and started to sway like a willow branch in a gentle breeze. The love-struck Roberts softly crooned about in the background of love and promises.

"Yes, I'd do anything for your love," she confirmed under her breath. Holly waited at the edge of her patience, wanting to indulge her basic urge to rip his gauzy tunic from his sumptuous chest. She was ready to please him, but mostly hoping to delight him.

"My Lady," he assured moving closer. "This is my only promise ... to love you gently, in your time."

Kaine's tender promise washed over her. His radiant eyes a testament he was telling the truth. He dropped his lips onto hers, his forceful kiss a symptom of his extraordinary love.

After exhausting the moment, Kaine took a thick, white bath towel, folded it twice, and laid it on the plush black area rug surrounding the deep, inviting pool of lavender-scented water. Kaine locked his loving gaze on her and took a tiny breath. The dreamlike moment had arrived. Kaine reached out to her. His long, thin fingers stroked the hollow of her cheek as if he were touching the delicate petal of a flower. Then his agile fingers untied the only thin ribbon on her snow-white gown that kept her body from his touch. With one urgent tug, the angelic cloth fell onto the black area rug.

Holly stepped over the pile of crumpled white fabric and moved closer.

Hook-by-hook, Kaine, unfastened the white satin and lace corset with ease and then tossed it next to the gown.

Holly stepped over the lingerie and moved closer. She stood a thread away from touching his body.

Kaine's gaze worshiped her, dressed only in a white thong. Her lean legs clad in white, silk thigh-high stockings. She wanted to shed her panties and stockings to crown the pile of useless clothes.

Kaine reached up and pulled out the hidden combs trapping her hair. The release of her curls and braids caused his eyes to flare with delight. He smiled a soft, satisfying grin while her long, russet hair cascaded all about her shoulders and then bounced to her waist. Kaine's breath fell into a rhythm that matched the blood racing in her veins.

The sudden depth of Holly's devotion for Kaine sent shivers rippling to her fingertips. She was thinking of thousands of ways to please him, to bring him pleasure and joy as he'd lavished on her.

Kaine's fingers cupped her chin as his thumb crossed over her bottom lip. He spoke in a whisper.

"I have looked into hundreds of thousands of eyes, but only in yours have I found my love, my future. You're the only woman who can build a brand new world with me. You, My Lady Love are a miracle."

His words were shocking, romantic and poetic, seeping into the wounded cavity of her heart as a healing ointment. He bent and kissed her again, but his sweet kiss barely satisfied the edge of her untamed needs. His lips strayed to her chin, and his tongue slid against the flesh of her throat.

A tiny moan escaped from her as he designed a moist path down to her chest.

His words were as silky. "I love the sweet taste of your skin. I love everything about you."

Drunk on his words, her eyes blazed with a passion for him as he kissed her neck down to the top of her shoulders. His fiery kisses made her ache and swell.

The gauze shirt obstructed her touch and she yanked at it.

"Take this off or I'll tear it off," she demanded. The cloth ripped against her excitement as she pulled it over his head. Kaine's beautiful dark hair fluttered in the air like feathers in a gentle wind and then settled, fanned about his shoulders, streaming down his broad chest.

"You're magnificent," she confessed as if stunned.

Like lightning, her fingers speedily wrestled the top button of his leather pants and then the zipper. She forced the supple, leather, down over his lean hips, setting the mystery of his love free. She pulled the tailored leather skin down each strong, lean leg to the floor. She dropped to her knees, yanking each boot and removed them. She slipped off his dark argyle socks and threw them aside

Kaine stepped out of his pants.

Sitting back on her haunches she looked up, admiring him, overwhelmed by his majesty, and whispered, "This My Lord is how I want you." The voice was sensual, one she didn't recognize. Her gaze wandered unabashedly about his perfect male body. He was soooo elegant.

Kaine smiled an almost shy smile before the powerful lust burst in his eyes screaming how much he wanted to devour her.

Holly moved nearer to him, rising up onto her knees, placing her cool hands on his warm thighs. She moved up his body, stopping every few inches to place an indulgent kiss to taste his skin. She hesitated at his growing arousal, to memorize every part of him. She fought the urge to taste him now. Instead, she watched him grow, moved closer, and kissed his skin all around him, honoring the beauty of his virility.

His fingers slipped into her hair and she smiled as tiny sounds escaped from his throat. She did not look up but focused where she was, planting kisses, more and more, along the valley of his smooth stomach. She moved beyond her knees, rising slowly, creating a sensual trail of warm, wet kisses up and, all over his broad, chiseled chest until she stood.

When she looked up into his eyes, his dreams shined as bright as the brigade of candlelight did.

The decision to continue her inventory, to know every inch of him, forced her to close her eyes. She committed to memory all of him, loving him and then dragged her lips up to his neck, kissing him, tasting him, moving up higher to his chin. All the while, her hands followed her kisses, creeping up his muscled chest, around to his back, bringing her loving touch of surrender. Her heart skipped. She sighed. Her breath almost exhausted as her body moved closer, so close his engorged desire, tempting her, rising to life.

Her magnificent Kaine was waiting for her, allowing her the time to become used to the blinding beauty of him growing full to pleasure her. She kissed his jaw line, moving closer, thirsting for him. She glanced up into his eyes then closed them.

His hands so powerful snaked along her back, pulling her closer still, lifting her up enough to dip his hot tongue into her waiting mouth, so ready to love him. He was searching her mouth for all the love she'd brought with her. He kissed her, biting her lower lip, nibbling as her lover, preparing her, so ready to release the wild spirit of his passion fighting to be set free.

"I love your lips, your hot tongue. I love your kisses. I love you, My Lady." He recited as if a promised vow, riding a steamy breath, as his hands let go of her.

Seconds later — a man named Kaine stood before her dressed only in his forever love for her.

Kaine stretched one arm beyond her to the marble countertop that lined the tub. Underneath, hidden from view, he pulled from a drawer, a long, pointed, knife, with red jewels encrusted in the handle.

"Do you still trust me?" he asked his voice eerie and throaty.

Her heart pounded with quick staccato beats. What was

Kaine doing?

"You don't know what I'm capable of doing. Haven't you heard stories about what rockers do with groupies?"

Holly bit her bottom lip, tasting the salty blood spill inside her mouth. Her hands were holding onto his strong, muscled forearms with the power of a vice grip, not knowing what to think.

"No ... and I'm not a groupie," she decided to utter in a tiny voice.

In a calm and reassuring tone, Kaine looked straight into her eyes and explained. "I know, all too well, I know. I want you to understand what you're getting into because it's so much more than these moments. You don't have any idea who I truly am. We are all alone here. I could tie you up My Lady, or force you to do things many times ... many ways. I could thrash you senseless, and I have enough money to keep it all quiet. Lady, you don't know who the bloody hell I am. Nevertheless, my intention is not to scare you, but it is a warning. I don't deserve you. Be certain, I'm no damned good for a sweet lady like you."

"You don't think very highly of yourself."

"Why should I? I know me. I've done horrible things that even frighten me. Things, I don't ever want you to know about or believe."

"You don't frighten me." She countered, raising her chin, trying to be brave, demanding her bottom lip to stop quivering.

"Maybe, I should."

"I trust you, Kaine," she admitted, commanding her body to relax in his arms.

"Maybe, you shouldn't. I am the chap your mother and father warned you about — the one to stay as far away from as you can."

"It is possible, you're right. However, I do trust you. How can I not love you? I've never seen or heard of what you speak. I've only known a wonderful, loving, sensitive man who puts my happiness before his, who speaks with words that shatter me, melting the core of my heart, my soul. How could I not trust and love you?"

He seemed to listen to her words with something more than reason.

"Those are the words I needed to hear, so badly. I have told you these things to caution you. The reputation I once had will shock you. Some continue to believe that is me. It will take a strong, invincible love for me to overcome what will come at you because you have chosen me. And for that reason, I am, so sorry since you don't know what you're seriously in for because you love me."

Her voice was silenced. She watched the passion flaring in his eyes, and they burned impatiently. This encounter had taken her by surprise. Again. His words, so unexpected, as if they were a test of her commitment, and they sapped the strength of her legs. The expression on his face said he was years beyond her experience. And then his words surprised her again.

"Never believe the rumors, the lies, the way things will appear. Always believe in me, trust me, but mostly, remember my true love for you." And then he kissed her a fierce, male dominating kiss, a protective kiss, from whatever it was, he knew was coming that terrified him. His tongue dove deeper, and his skills and passion brought her another wave of excitement, and anticipation, knowing this was only a prelude to the marvelous love that would soon follow.

Kaine broke away from her throwing his head back. His lips were wet, swollen, and hungry for her. She would never admit to him how much he had frightened her because he was right. He had driven his point home, making it painfully clear. They'd met two short days ago. She didn't know him and certainly, the world he lived in took no prisoners. She would have to dig deep because she did want to love him for such a long time, forever if he would have her.

"Don't move," he demanded. His voice laced with a new tone, smooth and dangerous.

She quickly remembered the knife and stood perfectly still holding her breath. She watched him intensely from the corner of her eyes. The blade gleamed like a mirror reflecting the bright candlelight. She watched Kaine laid the tip of the sharp blade against her hip. The tip dipped under the thong's elastic band, and the icy steel burned her hot flesh like a branding iron.

Kaine pressed it against her, and with one swift movement sliced through the thin strip of cloth holding up the thong.

He quickly cut the other side saying, "Last chance. Your choice. You're free to come to me." He smiled, the gleam in his eyes rewarding her for believing him, trusting him.

"I see you already trust me, and believe that I will never hurt you. It's true. I love you, so much it's alarming for so many reasons."

Holly hesitated to look up into his eyes, and when she did, there it was. His passion restrained. It told her it would not be long, but that there were still things he wanted her to know. He lavished her face with sweet, so sweet kisses as he pulled her down onto the thick towel. He stretched out beside her, filling every bend and curve of her body.

Still, haunting words flashed in her head.

I could force you....

He has a violent streak, especially with his girlfriends.

She drew her legs up with modesty, blanketed in the awareness of her nakedness with him.

Kaine moved closer and kissed her again. His hand glided up the outside of her body, avoiding all her erogenous zones. He continued to kiss her. To convince her she was safe with him. He told her repeatedly with his gentle touch that she could trust him, pushing any lingering fears away, and then vanished into the shadows.

Holly timidly started to touch him, lightly at first, and then more easily, roaming his soft, silken skin as her courage prescribed. Her hesitations were fading. She relaxed and explored him, filling the swells, and valleys of him, loving him, kissing him, deeper and deeper until she feasted on him.

His eagerness remained steadfast and pressed her abdomen. He moved in as close to her as his body would allow. The long, hard shape of him fought Kaine to have its way and enter her now.

Kaine's hand glided along the side of her body. He ran it down her thigh and over the top of the stocking to her knee. There he hooked his hand behind her knee and twisted her leg around his waist molding her to him. Unable to suppress a deep moan caught in his throat, Kaine pressed his lips on her neck.

He sent tiny quakes to ripple across her skin and she shivered.

"Closer. Come closer to me, My Lady Love. I want to feel the depths of you. You have smooth skin and curves. I love the soft, hot feel of you here." As he dipped his fingers inside her.

Again, his words, so unexpected.

"I need you — you're perfect — I want you, My Lady Love. For as long as you will have me."

His words of love wrapped around her and pulled her deeper into the spell.

He lowered his head and delivered a flurry of kisses along her neck moving toward her chest.

Between tiny breaths, she responded.

"That will be a long, long time my Precious One. But, it will be you that will quickly tire of me," she replied and closed her mouth over his.

"Never." She heard him say into her mouth.

He repeated, "Never."

Holly all but swooned, as she slipped her arms around his neck, anchoring her in his tremulous kiss. She flattened her breasts against his hot chest and sank into his embrace while his fingers moved magically inside her.

Kaine kissed her again, and again, catching short breaths between, and then kissed her again. He seemed to relish kissing her and then he kissed her again with a never-ending rush of kisses.

The stormy winds of her love rose swiftly within her. She quickly surrendered to Kaine's eager, lustful strokes, coming at her from everywhere.

He broke away, lost in his own windstorm of passion. He kissed her neck as he pulled his fingers from inside her, kissed the tops of her breasts, and quickly moved down to kiss her stomach. He drug his long dark hair across her body as if a wedding train of dark velvet.

She was spiraling out-of-control into a dark, bottomless pit of fiery, unquenchable love for him as she groaned louder.

Kaine moved, his kisses falling onto the tops of her thighs. His hair tickled her skin as he pulled himself up on his elbows. He paused and looked up at her.

She could barely see him. Her eyelids were heavy. But she caught a glimpse of the fiery lust, burning and flashing in his dark, blue, hungry eyes. He was coming for her with this act of love, so new, she'd never expected it from him, and now she longed for his touch.

A breath later, Kaine replaced where his fingers had been with his warm tongue. He brought the sacred kiss and awakened her, bringing her to life. Electricity couldn't have shocked her body more. He nudged her thighs apart to place his head closer. His warm, experienced tongue became more involved, more forceful. He licked between the lips stretching the flesh and sank into her satiny depth, where she waited hot and wet for him.

In another breath, he thrust his tongue inside her, and out, feeding on the sweetness of her, unleashing his talent, he lapped steadily on the tiny bud of her. He loved her, teased her, tantalizing her, and lured her to absolute ecstasy as he'd promised. He adored her, tugging, and sucking, showing her the way, alerting her that she was not far from the edge.

She drifted mindlessly from all the astonishing sensations

and grabbed a hand full of his hair, even pressing his face against her hips as he consumed her, hanging her suspended in time

Kaine loved her madly. Then slid up her moist body and hesitated. He looked daringly into her eyes, pulled open the black leather satchel leaning against the tub. He retrieved a small square foil from the pocket. He tore it open with his teeth, turned away to protect himself.

He looked back at her with gentle eyes, trying not to scare her with his powerful, sexual expectations. He inched his way up her body, various stormy emotions crossing his face.

What was he thinking?

Chapter Fourteen

SPELL I'M UNDER

He watched her every movement then asked in a low sultry voice. "Sure, you want me?"

She nodded yes, unable to understand how many times she would have to say she longed for him. Her patience wore thin and experienced a moment's incompetence to find words to prove beyond reason that her swelling breasts and the depth of her mysterious feminine softness waited as a hot furnace for him.

Kaine shifted the full weight of his body onto her as his thighs fit perfectly in-between hers.

Finally, he believed her. She welcomed him like petals of a flower opening to welcome the hot sun. His soft, warm hand caressed the side of her body, down to between her legs where his stiff eagerness pressed her. The heat of his panting on the side of her face ran raw and wild. When he moved and looked at her, she saw the hot joy of his love, bubbling in his eyes.

Whisked away by his swirling, storm of love, and out of her mind with eagerness, she smiled, ready to make her sentiments clear.

"Yes, I want you. Love me ... Kaine. Show me."

"As you wish ... My Lady Love, ... now," he promised. As if the gates of Eden opened, Kaine took both of his hands, cupped her derrière, and tightened his grip.

She was close, so close, to having all of him. She was hesitant to breathe.

Kaine pushed swiftly, at first, to gain immediate entrance as if to test the bonds of his commitment.

Holly, impatient, wanted more, to become his, needing all of him to fill her empty heart — now.

Kaine's wet, tender lips kissed her madly telling her ecstasy was seconds away from happening.

Overcome with scorching emotions, she wrapped fists full of his long dark silky hair around her hands and pulled him to her. Her mind broke. She fell from the edge, flying down into the wondrous essence of Kaine Walker. She wrapped her legs around his waist, grabbed hold of his body, and pulled him down with her into the depths of their erupting love, into a volcanic world where neither of them had ever been.

Holly heard ecstatic sounds rolling from her lips, cries of undeniable delight as Kaine pushed deeper. Simultaneously, bright bolts of lightning flashed about the castle. Kaine sank into her, pushing deeper. All around them, the demanding thunder tore into the plump rain clouds, ripping them apart.

The storm blasted violent sheets of water, whipping the castle walls mercilessly while Kaine kissed her zealously to the point of whimpering. Love-drenched sounds became commonplace.

She cracked open her eyes long enough to see him

watching, the flaring of lust deep in his dark blue eyes, his kisses growing more robust, thirsting for her.

She expected his kisses to become less urgent, but no, his kisses came faster and harder, his tongue filling her mouth, teasing her with what was to come.

He slipped his hands up behind her back as if to anchor him, and he molded his palms to the top of her shoulders and paused.

Finally, the magic moment had arrived.

With one swift motion, Kaine plunged his solid love to the top of her red-hot chamber.

A scream rip from her throat, riding the words that followed, confirming her profound pleasure. "Oh, my love, you feel amazing, so strong."

Fired by her admission, he let go, followed with another powerful thrust, and filled her.

Delirious with his plunging love, Kaine filled her. The deep, curling, throbbing abandon for him, burned hotter and deeper in her satiny heat.

He relaxed, and then sank deeper to an unfathomable depth inside her. His pleasure rolling from his lips each time he slammed into her pulled out and moved deeper again. Over, and over again, he moved, his strong muscles moving rhythmically under his skin. The maleness of him was commanding, bringing a wave, after wave, of unquenchable passion, setting her free to fly higher, as her pleasure increased, promising to pierce the universe.

She mystically floated into the open, welcoming the heart of Kaine, so open, so deep, and so loving. She was overcome with joy from his passion that ran so wild, and magical. It compelled her to open her heart wholly to the forever of him.

Holding him tighter, she wrapped her legs tighter around his waist, allowing him to sink deeper as they became one transcendent heartbeat. Their explosive and pulsating rhythm, reached a blazing crescendo, writing their forever love song. Deeper and deeper he thrust until she couldn't tell where she ended, and he began, becoming one as they arrived together in bliss.

He was panting, losing his control as he swallowed the sighs of her ecstasy with his sweet and loving kisses. He took all of her he could.

The force of the waves of bliss compelled her to hold him, anchoring herself to him, as she submitted to the burning, voracious, tremors drenching her, never wanting them ever to end. She hoped they'd continue, to explode, and explode, bringing her constant waves of exquisite fiery pleasure. She feverishly kept kissing him, lost in him, moving her hips with him, creating a new love with him — a love that had never existed before — a scorching and zealous forever love that would last them until the end of time.

He pressed his hands on her shoulders, pulled her to him again, again, and again. He moved so quickly. His body tensed. He arched his back and cried out loudly, "My Sweet, Lady Love."

He fought for his breath while trying to say.

"You're perfect, My Lady, stay with me, follow me." He directed with a breathy voice.

"Mmmm, my Precious One, anywhere." She swooned, twisting, taking it all from beneath Kaine. The maddening, pounding rhythm of their love song wasn't enough. She needed more of him. She uttered a piercing scream as she pushed her hips up to meet him, to take all of him. And she struggled to place her body in alignment, to swallow all of him inside her.

His hands slid down her moist body, then wrapped around her lower back. He lead her faster and faster along, building to frenzy — then dropped her off the edge of ecstasy.

She looked up into his beautiful, dark blue eyes, to see his devoted love, his hunger, the forever of Kaine. She smiled knowingly. He returned the acknowledgment. It was time. She let go, arching, crying out aloud, bursting into a blinding ecstasy then collapsed under him.

He quickly grabbed hold of her, wrapping his arms tighter around her lower back pulling her deeper into him as he invited her. "Now, together."

He, too, fell from the edge, his body convulsing, giving her all he had, leading her to bliss. He repeatedly groaned from somewhere deep inside him, and he took her with him.

Barely able to make out his words of love she listened to new promises he declared in her ear. The words followed by a succession of kisses he'd lavish there and then across her cheek. He moved quickly and covered her mouth as they drifted as one, in blissful joy, previously unknown to either of them. He showered her with affection. Seconds passed. Minutes passed. They added up to incredible moments of a perfect memory.

He held her derrière tightly in place.

Holly met his rhythmic thrust, no longer an unknown.

Kaine moved deeper inside her, thrusting in and out, deeper, and deeper, over, and over again, in and out, long, and deep until he could finally move no more.

She lay in complete submission, with him buried deep, so deep inside her, accepting his love, and lust, that shattered his every muscle, as he collapsed on top of her releasing another long raw groan. The same second her body transformed into shimmering liquid.

He dropped his mouth over her ear. His heavy pant tickled her skin as his hot quick breaths caressed her shoulder. He sank into her satiny depth for the last time, groaned again, as his heart pounded against her chest.

She floated, transcending time and space.

No, thoughts.

No knowing where she started and he ended, as they became one mind, one body, one soul, one love.

Her only wish; to stay wrapped about him like this forever, drifting in their forever love.

The smooth, soulful voice of Roberts was the only witness to the first of a thousand nights of their love together.

Holly lay dreamy-eyed, and lifeless, in his arms. She never wanted to move. Then, she discovered, she couldn't move. Then, there was no need to move. His passionate and dynamic lovemaking left her spellbound and set her free. And so mesmerized by him, she believed no other man existed in the world. Kaine Walker had placed her under his ineffable love spell, and with the strength of a newborn bird.

She whispered, "... I ... love you ... my Precious One ... forever."

He kissed her ear, cheek, and then raised his head to kiss her lips, so softly, loving, and then he tenderly confessed.

"I love you too, My Lady Love. Maybe three or four ... I

love you a thousand times," louder each time he acknowledged as if to announce it to the world.

I love you too, My Lady Love, maybe three or four. I love you a thousand times.

She repeated the words in her mind, drugged from the heady words, and lost in his joyful vow.

His limp, heavy body covered hers. His head rested in the crook of her neck. His breath coming hard and fast, as the last of his arousal slowly withdrew from her body.

Time evaded her.

He gradually moves beside her and collapsed.

The coolness of the evening settled on her wet, love-drenched body. When she opened her eyes, it wasn't entirely clear if she had been in a deep trance and dreaming. She turned her head and forced her eyes open a bit more, and the first beautiful vision that greeted her was the dim glow of the candlelight reflecting his love sparkling in his eyes.

There he was.

The man.

Kaine.

Chapter Fifteen

LOVE ME DO

Kaine Walker was not a man of international wealth and fame with a reputation for violence and debauchery. She'd found a sensitive, reflective, and poetic man. The man who had created all of this pleasure for her to bring her happiness.

Kaine was lost in his mysterious thoughts. Was he thinking the same as her? Did he wonder how they had been this lucky, this fortunate to find each other? How much of a miracle their love was?

Holly closed her eyes lost in thoughts of him, all his amazing talents, and devoted skills to love her. He'd understood how it had been for her to be away from making love. He'd been so patient and creating this beautiful fairy tale fantasy for her had made him her champion. Apparently, his leagues of women had not dulled his sense of love, and romance. Lust was something that had been common for him. He'd explained he'd been alone for so long. He didn't want sex that was plentiful in his world. He'd had all of his erotic fantasies, and fantastic dreams fulfilled hundreds of times over the years. Yet, it was here in this castle, love caught up with him, in the magic of their love.

For those reasons, it must have been surprising to him to learn that instead of his love for her being his strength, he saw it had become his vulnerability. He'd confessed to feeling afraid something outside their private inner sanctum would pull them apart. His warning so frightening it served its purpose. To love Kaine Walker would not be as easy as it had been there with the world shut out, alone to celebrate their lust and their budding love.

She loved him even more, realizing what he had done for her, to nurture their growing love. He'd known what was coming, and he was right, she needed to trust him, let him work it out because she had no idea how to prepare. Where was Rock Star Girlfriend 101 in the schedule of university courses? And if there had been one, she would have certainly never signed up for the class. She looked over to her romantic time traveler ready to move in close to him and begin again, dreaming of starting with his toes and working her way up to his scrumptious lips.

"Bloody, Hell! I forgot! Holly! The tub!"

Kaine's frantic cry jerked from her bliss. She joined Kaine in a swift, hearty laugh as he sprinted to turn off the bubbling water. It threatened to crash over the sides any second and drench them. He sat beside her laughing.

How much she loved his deep, boisterous laugh, and she vowed to bring him nothing but laughter and happiness for the rest of his life. She'd wanted love. A man's love and she'd received more than she'd ever dared bargain for from this magnificent man. She had Kaine's, an energetic, robust, and thrilling man's love.

Then thoughts of the future arrived — followed by the foreverness, creeping in silently, the wants of a home, children — his children, his home, his nights. If he'd only ask her now, she'd accept his proposal before he was able to speak the last word. He didn't seem opposed to her having a career but it would always be there. But to raise a family with Kaine was what she knew she wanted in her future more than anything in the world. She could only hope their road together would fulfill her fantastic dream.

Kaine slid back into her embrace and pressed his body against her. He kissed her again. His hot, seducing tongue probed her mouth, while he lifted her one leg at a time, removed her garters and then silk stockings.

He took her hand and guided it behind his neck.

She understood and held onto his shoulders as he lifted her up into his arms.

He struggled to stand and gain his balance, but his strong arms lifted her up high, higher until he stood straight and proud. Kaine hesitated, indulged himself, kissing her, biting, and pulling on her wet swollen lips. When he'd had enough, he stepped into the steamy, cleansing water and sat her down straddling his lap.

Dizzy from his loving display she spoke softly.

"You sure know a lot about a woman's fantasy."

"I promised you and I don't break my promises."

"No, you don't. You're a man of honor, Kaine Walker. You have remembered every tiny detail. It seems you have Mother Nature charmed. She indulged and spoiled you in your every whim. She made the lightning flash boldly and the thunder roll, while the rain pounds violently against the castle walls as if a scene straight out of a gothic novel."

"All to please you, My Lady Love, all for you," Kaine boasted, smiling appreciably, then kissed her again, long and lingering.

His inexhaustible kisses were stealing her breath away, persuading her to believe his words. Her tender nipples rubbed against Kaine's hard chest as she tried to get as close to him as possible. All the while, the omnipotent thunder crashed about the skies causing the sunken to tub vibrate.

The lavender scented water lapped about her as she thought about Kaine's magnificent loving. He'd surpass any dreams she'd ever dare imagine. She slid her hand about Kaine, moving freely all over his smooth, oiled skin, then relaxed in his arms, resting her head on his shoulder to stop her head from spinning. And she hoped it wasn't too soon to want him inside again.

"I forgot one thing," he spoke deep from the hollow of his chest.

"Impossible. What more could I take from you," she asked in a satisfied tone.

"Not you, My Lady. Me. I'm hungry." He chuckled as he cocked his head, and then charmed her by lifting an eyebrow. He playfully bit into her neck and predicted. "You must be too."

Holly's hand slipped from his muscled shoulder and plunged deep into the warm bubbling water. She turned to face him. She slid her hand down his abdomen until her fingertips touched him where his majestic power lay resting. She watched his eyes closing as if enjoying her loving devotion. All she wanted was him. It was so overwhelming to want him again, more of him, all of him, now, inside her, with all he had.

She decided to risk telling him. "This is all I want or need from you." As she delicately traced his shape with long, spirited movements, her eyes barely open. "I'm hungry too, and you know how the saying goes ... for you. Your body's so soft. But, when you grow hard, you make me want you more than I ever possibly dreamed." She conceded as she continued to stroke him until he was strong, and hard again in her hand.

"I didn't ...I didn't know I could want you so badly, so quickly."

Kaine smiled, softly at first, then broadened his lips to wear a sunny, satisfied smile almost as if amused by her words, and coaxed her closer.

"Come to me, girlfriend. You understand why I have been insisting that you never, ever leave me. I knew we would have a powerful and explosive recipe, mixing love with lust and then sex. I knew if I didn't rush you, we would be like this and imagine My Lady, we've only begun. I can't conceive of you ever being away from me."

She moved her head to agree.

"I do ... I understand now, and I promise I will never leave you. Not until the last sunrise." She affirmed in full agreement. How could she ever leave a man that could make her soar the way he did? No dream had prepared her for where Kaine could take her, how he would take charge and own her every sense. There was no way she would ever live without him, and with that admission, she experienced an enormous amount of relief; convinced her yearning to love Kaine would burn forever.

Kaine kissed her quickly before he aired his thoughts. "I was worried if I broke my promise, and didn't wait until you were ready to accept all of me, my experience might scare you. Then you may never let me touch you, and allow me to love you the ways I want. I am happily pleased to know that you have a strong appetite for me and that you enjoyed being with me, as much as I have with you. There's so much more to making love. For most, this marks the end of the night, but for me, it's merely the beginning. I will teach you many things because your body can experience more pleasure."

Holly was impressed with her skilled lover's road map to love. "I can take all the pleasure you can give me. I am eager to learn, and I am ready because you took the time. If you have any last doubts my Precious One, I will erase them. I love your constant touch, your rhythm, and experience, your sweet love, and then your intense love. And oh, your kisses, how they keep coming. And after I have learned what pleases you, I will never get enough of you, especially deep inside me."

She pulled back to see if his face showed any surprise at her boldness. She wondered if he saw the rosy flush in her cheeks from the flaring heat that pricked her skin. She did not recognize this new creation speaking, this transformed woman so in love.

Kaine swept her tighter into his arms, and she came as close to fainting as she'd ever been.

"You're so perfect for me ... for so many reasons." He swore and groaned again with pleasure. He easily took hold of her milking hand, to stop his swelling before he emptied his seed, and cast it adrift in the water. He pulled away trying to control his breathing and looked into her eyes. His heavily hooded lids warned to brace herself. Another bombshell was on its way.

She was right.

"Tell me about Brett. Must I slay him to keep the hand of the fair maiden?"

She choked back a surprised laugh and nonchalantly replied.

"Not much to tell. He's rich, spoiled, and ....."

Kaine cut her off mid-sentence. "Madly in love with you as I am? Say I have a chance?" His words begged, his face smiling.

Madly in love with you as I am?

It took her a moment for the picture of Brett to focus in her mind. No, Brett was not madly in love with her. And she was about to tell Kaine when she saw the glint in his eyes. She caught onto the game, she coyly added. "Maybe, just maybe, you have caught the tiniest bit of my attention."

"Tell me, where is Lord Brett? That I might please, My Lady. I can behead this evil rival of mine."

"I couldn't possibly tell you that. He's out slaying dragons."

"Does he slay any of them for you?"

Holly stopped the game. Kaine had unwittingly done it again and thrown chilled water on her beautiful fantasy. A cold reality burst in, forcing Holly to concede that Brett never did anything for her, except keep her near him. He'd kept her exceedingly busy, smothering her with demanding tasks. She did not love Brett, no passion, just the invisible bond of gratitude. She'd bet he'd agreed he'd been trapped in a life-strangling obligation of a long forgotten promise.

Holly's face must have revealed her distress because Kaine suggested with mounting concern as if he was losing interest and didn't want to continue the game.

"The evil Brett does not favor My Lady? She will no longer give him her attention?"

She forced a smile, trying to forget Brett. Kaine was such a dear to attempt to give her a fairy tale night she had asked for earlier. She placed her water-wrinkled hand on his cool, pale cheeks and kissed his lips quickly.

"Yes, My Lord. However, there's another, a magnificent, dark-haired man, a devastatingly, handsome, and mysterious prince. The dark prince stole my heart, my every thought, my body, and soul."

She looked directly into his eyes, hoping to ease his concerns by showing him how much she adored him.

Kaine squirmed a bit.

She knew this trick. He was about to change the subject again. She released a solitary breath. She was trying to repair the broken bridge to his heart.

Had she made him uncomfortable?

Said the wrong thing?

"My Lord, what is your pleasure? You need only ask. Your wish will always be my command."

Chapter Sixteen

SAVING ALL MY LOVE FOR YOU

Kaine flatly stated, "I'm going downstairs and check the fridge."

Holly cocked her head a bit taken aback by his response but accepted the game had ended.

Then, as if he would never see food again, with a lighter joking tone Kaine added, "I'll be back with provisions."

"Bring a lot. You're going to need to regain your strength." She instructed, deciding to let his mood pass and missed him already.

Kaine laughed naughtily as he threw back his dark hair. The wet tips clung to his shoulders. His sexy gaze settled on her face, and he reminded.

"I haven't begun to awaken you my sleeping beauty." His cool, breezy tone assured.

The saffron light from the candles splintered magically in his eyes. Love dusted them, telling her that he looked forward to keeping his word.

She slid onto the seat beside him in the tub relieved everything was perfect between them.

He stood. He was physically superb. His body a perfect carving of what a man like him would be. He stepped out of the soapy water. His nakedness captured her imagination as she anticipated endless pleasures to come.

"Brr..." Kaine announced to the inky darkness that surrounded them. Then he shoved his arms into a plush black, velvet robe while slipping his feet into lambswool lined leather slippers. He bent over, picked up the black satchel, and briskly crossed the auditorium-sized suite to vanish into the dark shadows that skirted the outer edge.

Holly shivered. It was instantly cold and lonely without him. She listened to Roberts sing a strong pledge of sentiment. His melodic voice filled her, knowing whenever she heard these love songs, she would remember this brilliant night of raw passion and pure love with Kaine. She leaned over the tub and searched the drawer for matches to relight the gutted candles. Roberts sang about the foreverness of love for the third time, surprising her that it had it been such a long while that they had made love.

Kaine returned majestically piercing the darkness, so reminiscent of the Hard Rock video. He stood next to her holding a large bottle of mineral water, and a shiny, silver platter of sliced chicken breasts with sprigs of parsley, attractively arranged around the edges. The next inner ring displayed plump orange, and ripe, red, apple slices mixed with large, succulent, grapes. In the center was an assortment of cubed cheeses. He set the elegant serving wear on the thick ledge of the black marble tub.

Holly looked up at him. His haunting, blue eyes were watching her. His head bobbed like his neck was on a spring, keeping time to the music.

"This is how I feel Holly. I want to be your forever man, and I hope you will be my forever woman."

"I'm yours as long as forever is, my Precious One," she promised, slipping her hand over his to set the mood for more romance.

Kaine had smiled appreciatively seconds before he dropped his robe to the floor. The soft glow of the scented candles highlighted his smooth, streamlined features like an exquisitely carved statue. Kaine was unmistakably one hundred percent flesh-and-blood man. His body had a light dusting of manly hair, mostly on his chest. She allowed her gaze to drift to the part of him that had loved her and sent her to paradise. How beautifully shaped he was, with the hair cropped short, and she longed to taste him. Though she'd never performed the act of love, he'd driven her to abandonment from the ways his warm tongue loved her and understood he would eventually expect her to reciprocate.

She wanted to find the perfect inspiration to please him because to bring him pleasure, was her single purpose. On the heels of his astonishing lovemaking, she filled with cravings to indulge him in his every fantasy. She was eager to satisfy Kaine, with a longing and deep, burning, Hell, call it wickedness.

Kaine sat on the ledge, dangling his legs in the water, indulging his appetite for cheese and gave special attention to a plump slice of orange. She swam to the front of him and raised herself up onto his thighs. She slipped the pads of her fingertips on the back of his neck and pulled his head down to kiss him. As she ran her tongue along the seam of his lips, he tasted of sweet orange. She found the opening of his mouth and dipped into his sweetness.

His kiss left her heady. She pulled away to look at his body. She promised herself, she would taste every inch of his flesh before the sun rose, knowing she would never be free of this longing for him.

The silence stretched long between them.

With one thing on her mind, she followed the compelling notion of kneeling on the floor of the tub before him as if in front of a sacred altar. She reached over and kissed his chest, allowing her lips to trail down to where her hand lay next to his resting sex. She leaned in to trace the tip of him with her tongue. She quick experienced a jolt of his body. When her tongue touched him again, a groan escaped from his throat. She dared to taste him, running her tongue along the length of him. He promptly swelled, inviting more of her touch. How soft he was — how hard he became. She parted her lips to take him in, and he tasted of lavender. His ever-growing shape increased, larger and larger with each passing interval to full size. She found it difficult to adapt more of his demanding shape inside her mouth, and placed one hand around him, and the other rested on his slender thigh to caress him ever so lightly.

All past doubts and hesitation vanished as Kaine filled her mouth again. She moved her lips, her tongue, hoping to delight and pleasure his full size. She pressed closer to him, the essence of the lavender scented oil, now mixed with his musky scent, climbed sweetly into her memory. Fired by sucking him in deeper in her mouth, she was a bit lightheaded. Her body shuddered with shattering tremors, threatening to drag her quickly along the path to ecstasy and arrive before him. She tried to deny the sexual quakes slamming into her where red–hot convulsions lined up, ready to blow her away. She commanded her body to keep it together and finish making noisy, pleasurable love to him. To take him with her, before she gave in first, released him and be forced to scream out in unbearable pleasure, and collapse in his lap.

She focused on pulling Kaine deeper into her mouth trying to keep up the frenzied, rhythmic pace of her lips, sucking while he dug his fingers into her hair. She was so close, but without warning, her head jerked back with a sharp pain, and his hands pulled harder when the pain should end.

But it didn't.

He wrapped locks of her hair around his fingers and pulled again. Kaine tilted her head back, maybe, not realizing how much it hurt, ripping her mouth off his rock hard length.

Kaine released his hand, her hair, and his erupting groans of praise empowered and fueled Holly. Her resolution set to return and love his beautiful, hot sex like no other because she carried the only hope he had — her love.

In a feverish frenzy, she sucked him in deeper and harder until she pulled entrenched groans of pleasure from his throat. He lost control, and his release arrived, pouring his warm seed into her mouth.

The warmth flooded her mouth and she swallowed quickly, pulled back, and looked up to find him watching her intensely. She'd hoped to please him. However, to see his dark, lusty eyes while she held him purposefully in her mouth was more daring than she'd expected. The interlude was powerfully sexy and compelled her to suck harder.

As the inner furnace of her body built to a volcanic crescendo, she closed her eyes and released a thick moisture to drain down her inner thighs quickly to dissolve in the water. She heard the raucous sounds of her own release rise high in her throat, and she opened her eyes.

How beautiful Kaine looked with the candle's golden glow on his face. She closed her eyes, taking the picture of him enjoying his release. The moans pouring from him were satisfying. She'd succeeded.

Holly sat waiting for the dizziness to subside but pleased she had given her man the same intense pleasure he'd lavished on her. She moved away, a few inches in front of him, to gaze on his gorgeous face sheathed in the success of her new talent.

She'd anticipated his encouragement.

Wait — she did not feed on pleasure from his face. No, his facial expression produced a hard, serious glare. His eyebrows were pinched, and his eyelids narrowed. He wasn't reeling from the trip to bliss. She watched the dark thoughts cross his eyes, once a flicker of distaste, rapidly growing into repulsion.

Her heavily hooded eyelids wore the glaze of a woman lost in love. What's more, the thick taste of her Precious One was on her lips, in her mouth, as she swallowed. She considered if it was wise to ask why his mood was changing. She worked her way up his waning shaft. She stopped, licked the top of him dry, released him, and tried to calm her breath. She spoke quietly, and cautiously.

"Have I displeased you, My Lord?"

Kaine remained silent, moved to enter the cool water,

sliding in like a Water Moccasin snake to her side. He placed his head back, dragging his hair along the ledge. He raked his fingers through the front of his hair, pulling it behind him as if to give himself time to compose his thoughts, body, and emotions after his release into her mouth.

His silence was scaring her, and she didn't like it one bit.

After one long, frightening pause, Kaine leaned over to nibble affectionately on the bottom of her earlobe. After another long segment of indulging himself, sending masses of tingling sensations all over her body, as if to put her at ease, he pressed his lips against her ear and confronted her. "Where did you learn to do that?" A cold, biting edge was in his tone of voice.

Thinking he must be playing the game. She giddily threw her head back. She smiled smugly, and then glanced over at her devilishly, striking Kaine, not wanting to point out her inexperience, hoping not to have disappointed him, and dared to say, hoping for no reprisals.

"You don't have to teach me everything."

Kaine's expression tightened around his suspicious eyes. His tone of voice level, and laced with a harshness she would never expect from him. Especially now!

"I understand how you have kept Brett away from you." The indictment was hard and fast.

Holly sat back, stunned. What would make Kaine think of Brett now?

"Well, I have a past, Kaine." She produced, deciding whether she should tell him this act of love was not something she'd given any man. She trailed off, not sure how much to explain, questioning if she needed his personal instructions on how to please him.

Kaine's blue eyes grew dark, stormy, and then hard, matching his cold, icy, voice. "I also understand now. You used your mouth to satisfy Luka."

Not a question — an accusation.

"Luka?" She blurted out astonished and almost choked repeating his name, while her eyebrows lifted, registering surprise. Luka didn't have the time for her to make love with him in this intimate way. Then again, this wasn't the time to mention that!

"Why would you speak of Luka now?"

But Kaine stopped listening. He recoiled, and struck with the icy burn of jealousy. "What happened between you and Luka in the dressing room?"

"Why do you ask?"

"Because I believe more has passed between the two of you than you want me to find out. I know Luka. He is not as patient a chap as I am."

"What exactly do you want to know? Ask me, I'll never lie to you, Kaine."

"Has he kissed you? Has he touched you? That's what I want to know Holly. That's all I want to know," he demanded again. His voice full of anger trailed into disgust.

Holly sat quietly. Thinking. Clearly, the game was over, and she could kick herself. She realized if she told the complete truth, including her morning with Luka at the hotel, Kaine would hit the roof. If she lied, there could be no real trust grow between them and the basis of their relationship grew from her lying. Luka would make sure and enjoy, letting the cat out of the bag. Why did he have to ask her this?

Especially now?

"It's ... not what you think." She insisted, as a tiny offering.

"I think many things when you're silent. You're *my* girlfriend. I thought Luka knew better than to touch what is mine."

"What am I hearing? Did you call me something less than human? I'm a possession of yours? Your property? Wake up Kaine, this is the twentieth century!" She shouted at him looking for a word to describe his outburst. But the only word that came to mind was an old, outdated word, chauvinistic. Still, his words had pierced her like a dagger, stabbing at her repeatedly.

From nowhere, she saw the blood. Instead of giving in to her fears, anger stirred inside her as a snake shifting its coils, and she screamed at him.

"Apparently, I was wrong about your knowing a lot about women."

"What do you mean?" He challenged, with an accusatory tone.

She stood. The fading candlelight threw a twin of her movements on the wall in the form of harsh shadows.

She snapped, yelling at him loudly, forcing his head to bend backward.

"Don't you take that tone with me," she shot back.

Kaine's body stiffened as he sat in the water. His jaw clenched and the glare in his eyes was burning like Hell's fires. He commanded an answer. "What did Luka mean when he said *he* dressed you, Holly?"

"Just that. He came into my dressing room and helped me get out of an awful corset because I was late and due on the set. He didn't like the costume. So, he had Lilly bring the gown," she quickly countered. Her voice shaky, as it sank in, knowing she was lying by omission because her indiscretion with Luka was so close to being revealed.

Kaine quickly filled in the blanks. "I'm not stupid, Holly. I understand you. You allow him to see you naked, touch you. Why? Why do you continue to let him touch you, Holly? Why do you like his touch? Why do you enjoy the way he looks at your body? Do you miss the way his hands touch your skin? Do you know that every time I see you look into his eyes, it tears me up inside, and I lose a part of you to him? Is that why?"

Each question of his interrogation increased an octave until he was shouting at her. His questions hurled so fast, he confused her.

She couldn't answer him because she didn't know why. Then the desperate, and the tormented look in his eyes arrived that said her actions crushed his heart. They were intense and piercing. Luka's words returned with deadly speed.

His jealousy will destroy any possible feelings for you.

Kaine wouldn't let up. He badgered her and the muscles and veins in his neck strained to pop.

"Did you want to kiss him, Holly? Did you?"

Holly was dying inside, leaving every emotion flattened. Her new, loving, feelings for Kaine put to the test. As painful, his words felt she didn't know what to say to stop him. Instead of giving him comfort, her words blasted out before she could stop them.

"Yes, Kaine. Yes, I wanted to kiss Luka. And when I did, I...."

"When you what? You have kissed Luka and professed to love me? Holly?"

"Kaine, you're mixing things up, it's no secret I met Luka first."

"You know I mean today. I'll rephrase it, counselor."

His sarcasm was thick, his eyes hard. The eyes of the stranger, he truly was.

"Did you kiss Luka after the press called you *my* girlfriend or to be even clearer after you knew we would spend this night here?"

Hot tears sprang to her eyes because of being caught in an awful web that quickly sucked her down into the mire of suffocating guilt. The truth of her betrayal wove an unshakable grasp. The more she fought to be free, the tighter the web of deceit wrapped around her. She searched her mind for a reasonable explanation. Unfortunately, the look in his eyes demanded to know that second, which one of them did she love?

She didn't know anymore.

"Yes, Kaine, after the press, and after I knew I was staying here with you," she finally admitted, choosing the truth, hoping it wouldn't cost her everything, leaving her every effort to keep her bottom lip from quivering.

Holly stood up straight and stared down into his eyes.

"Is that what you wanted to hear me say? No wonder Luka said he might as well kiss me. He said your jealousy would make you believe he did anyway. Said, he might as well enjoy what it was you would accuse him of, and he did."

Holly glanced away taking with her the image of Kaine's white-hot, angry, expression as it drained his face. She peeked back to see him drop his chin to his chest as if beaten. His hair fluttered about his head like a dark waterfall.

From somewhere deep in his throat, she heard his words, gaining momentum like a bitter wind, and they hit her with utter disbelief.

He looked directly into her eyes and accused her in a thick, disgusting tone.

"You wanted to fuck him? Didn't you, Holly?"

The Kaine she knew vanished. This man was cool, distant, with piercing black eyes that looked right through her.

"What sort of a woman are you? Are you Luka's whore?"

He vented, clearly betrayed. Then stood defiantly and stepped out of the tub. He threw her a disillusioned glance as he bolted toward the door.

Holly's whole body trembled with betrayal. She didn't know why she followed him. With each step Kaine took away from her, she wanted to explain he was ripping her heart out. However, her white-hot anger stopped her, blocking the redeemable words from pouring forth. Instead, to her horror, she heard herself screaming.

"Yes, ... yes. I wanted to fuck him, as you so crudely put it because he treats me like something special. Do you hear me, Kaine Walker? Luka makes me feel good, so fucking good..."

She screamed at him as she kicked the towel bunched on the floor.

"So fucking good..." Her words trailed between sobs.

But Kaine couldn't hear the last of her words over her anguished cries. Her tears burst forth riding a torrid river of pain, cascading down her cheeks making her madder. She sobbed deeply, filled with regret, and responded.

"I didn't mean it, Kaine," she wailed and collapsed into a ball on the plush, black area rug.

Kaine continued to walk away.

"I didn't mean it ... I'm your whore."

Her voice was small now, repeating one word between her sobs.

"Kaine ... Kaine ... Kaine..."

He could not hear her after the door slammed shut.

Chapter Seventeen

TEARS IN HEAVEN

*S*omewhere *between darkness and dawn, blood dripped.*
A ragged gash forced the warm, crimson, blood to ooze
from her pale flesh. She watched the blood trickle,
etching a sparkling, crimson web down her thin ivory palm.
Death crept closer to applaud her decision. It stood a breath
away from her. The cold, coiled finger under her chin gently
lifted. She glanced into the cracked mirror. It was such a
pretty face with graveyard eyes.

Holly moved, rolled over on the floor, and opened her eyes
Darkness.

Had she drifted off in a dream?

Yes, and the vile dream followed her, haunting her. She
started to sob, trading her fleeting joy for grief. She crawled
off the area rug, moving toward the main room. She stopped,
laid on the cool, polished, brick floor, fighting the memory of
what she had tried to do the last time her lover had left her.
The memory so real, it scared the hell out of her. Her cheek

resting against the coolness of the smooth, cold, stone floor reminded her. The memory all too clear, her red, red blood flowing freely from her wrists onto her pure white wedding dress. Yes, she had wanted to die, so long ago.

With a new hole growing in her chest where her heart once flourished, she wanted out for a second time because the searing agony made her believe death would stop the pain. She no longer cared that she lay naked on the cool floor. Why would she care how her body was found?

Where were the razor blades?

Her thoughts dictated she pulled herself upright to stand and search the spa area for a basin. That was the first time Holly noticed the rest of the room because she had been, so involved with Kaine. The thought of his abandonment brought a new wave of disparity with hot tears to follow. She wiped away the drops that flowed with the ease of a child's and looked around out of the spa area.

Only the corner spa area, of the giant room, remained lit by the lingering candles and made it difficult to see the other walls. What secrets awaited her discovery?

She picked up a lit stub that had once been a long, slender candle and set out to explore the apartment and discovered a generous sitting area she'd once heard they called it in England. She saw a well-worn, black leather couch, and chair. Scattered about were vintage clocks and tables, a deep blue, velvet settee, the biggest she'd ever seen.

Along another wall, she made out a fireplace once meant to keep the mammoth room warm seemingly restored to its original enchantment and splendor. She pictured the room being the sleeping quarters of English noblemen. As she moved closer to the mantel, she noticed the top of the thick, Old English scrolled, wood was bare as if overlooked with a thin layer of dust. There weren't any pictures hung on the walls, no small frames of family photos, or books of any sort, anywhere. There wasn't any place to hang clothes unless that was why there was an enormous armoire. Who was the man that lived here? He shares nothing of himself with the castle.

The oak paneled walls were in excellent repair, oiled and shiny. The ceiling was ornate and magnificently painted, etched with more Old English scrolling. However, the apartment was empty. Whoever lived there was more unhappy than she.

Time crept along and eventually her idle thoughts of suicide disappeared. She pulled her thick, wet, hair over her shoulder, and braided it down the front while wandering back to the tub area. She picked up Kaine's black, velvet robe and slipped her arms into the damp sleeves, and straight into the intoxicating, scents of him that quickly awakening her arousal followed by an immediate heat and longing for him.

She closed her eyes and pulled the robe to close around her half-expecting he'd of cooled off, and returned. She didn't know if she should be concerned or wait?

Unfortunately, she didn't know anything.

New feelings appeared as lightning bolts filling her with boiling anger for thinking so, irrationally. No one was worth losing her life over, no one. The doctors at the hospital had warned her never to act on her impulses. To wait, think about what to do in the situation then call someone. No longer in immediate despair, she noted she was depressed enough to want to talk anyone … someone.

How? A phone.

She remembered seeing one next to the leather couch and hurried over to pick up the receiver. It was then Holly discovered how truly alone she was.

Line dead.

Lightning flashed.

The thunder rolled, again, and again, and again.

The lightning crashed wildly.

The violent storm squashed the last of her feelings of safety. She trembled, jumping at each crash of lightning, and the jarring roll of the thunder. The fierce storm had surrounded her, threatening the safekeeping of the castle. She sat on the side of the couch. Her nerves shot. She nibbled at the edges of her fingernails nervously. Where the hell was Kaine? Was he anywhere near her? Left in this frightful castle all alone had not been in her brochure of London's hottest spots.

Then it struck her. Could it be she was utterly alone? Maybe Kaine had dressed and taken off on the bike? No, that didn't make any sense. Why would he risk his safety in the storm to abandon her? She knew she sounded paranoid, but then she hadn't understood much about Kaine lately, bringing it all home again. Kaine wasn't much more than a stranger to her.

As ridiculous, as that statement sounded, the fact remained that Kaine was her boyfriend. She hadn't had one of those for seven years. It would seem they'd had their first fight, and what a doozy. She'd have to remember that Kaine brooded, his feelings, so ultra-sensitive but they fueled his genius that made him the best award winning singer and songwriter in the world. It also pulled all the emotions out of his audience. He was Kaine, a creative man, and a spectacular lover, and this was only the beginning of their long road together.

The thunder rolled again.

He was in the castle — somewhere.

She could sense him....

The moment of decision arrived.

That's it!

With no wish to spend, any more time in the hospital trying to heal her pain. She vowed she wouldn't lose another lover because it had been too unbearable previously.

It was time.

She decided to find Kaine to forge a path to understanding each other. If he couldn't, then she would leave when the storm allowed.

At least, she had an alternative plan.

Chapter Eighteen

MISS YOU

Holly screamed in the dark corridor of her mind. "Damn you, Luka Hunter! You're trouble when you're near me. You're trouble when you're miles away in London."

She raised her fist and shook it in protest to the air. The crushing grief in her chest verified her heart breaking. She placed her head in her hands, squeezing her eyes closed and cried out sending an echo.

"Have I lost the Precious One?"

She didn't know how much time had passed since Kaine decided to vanish.

"Kaine you're such a brat! A spoiled, selfish brat...." She'd spat to the chilly draft. They were the last of her words hurled toward the path Kaine made before he'd slammed the door. It no longer mattered if he heard her.

Another long stretch of time passed. Mother Nature apparently as unhappy as Holly pounded on the narrow-shaped windows in the luxurious prison. Holly busied herself with draining the tub. Afterward, she shivered from the cool air concerned why the thermostat wasn't working. She nibbled on pieces of tasteless cheese and soggy fruit.

Where the hell was Kaine? The candles surrounding the tub burned dangerously low, and one by one gutted and died. The long shadows jumping on the wall near the tub told her there was little time left. Soon, each flame would struggle to remain alive. It wouldn't be long before she would not only be utterly alone but forsaken in darkness.

She waited for his footsteps....

It had been a long time since Kaine stomped out of the room. Her anger cooled transforming into boredom then curiosity.

Holly selected the longest candle. Tired of Roberts coaching her to do anything for love, she wandered to the edge of the darkness and found the doorway.

Darkness.

Spooky.

Her sightline restricted to the extremely black area stretching ten feet in front of her. The lightning slowed and the thunder calmed a bit.

Holly loudly called out Kaine's name. Her voice returned from the hollow, empty castle halls. The last candle she held fought the flood of red melting wax. The wick danced valiantly, struggling to stay alive, and then flickered, and died.

"Damn!"

Cast into sudden darkness, Holly filled with a black horror of despair. Lost, she blundered down the corridor. As she saw it, she had two choices; wait or go find Kaine. She said in a feisty tone into the darkness, "Damn you, Kaine. I didn't come five thousand miles to lose you now."

Holly inched her way along, placing her hands in front of her like a blind woman reaching out to touch the rough shell of the castle wall, so like Kaine. Step-by-step, she moved cautiously down the long corridor closer to him.

Her heartbeat raced at twice its normal rate, and she could only hope she was heading in the direction of the stairs. The lightning flashed again separating the clouds and brought bright patches of light to spread along the long, darkened corridor. She welcomed the light showing her a path to the top of the stairs. She followed them down three flights to the ground floor. A driving wind violently blew open a window above her making a loud, frightening, crashing sound.

She jumped and screamed, "Damn!"

Her cry of fear was carried away on the freezing wind. She leaned on the cold, spiny wall to collect herself. The lightning flashed again, and the thunder rolled heavily, leaving her trembling in total fright.

Then she wished a dangerous thought.

She wished Luka were with her.

Oh, why had she sent him away?

Holly couldn't forget Luka. He'd become the source of her growing problems with Kaine, but somehow, she didn't think he would abandon her. He would have stayed, held her, and consoled her. At the minimum made love to her again and again until the storm passed. She hated these kinds of storms. It was during a violent one like this she almost lost her life when she'd forced the blood to drip from her wrists.

She blocked the dreadful thoughts from her mind and focused on something to make her feel safe. Right on cue that thought produced images of lingering in Luka's warm, strong, arms, protectively holding her. She recalled gazing into his fucking blue eyes-to-die-for that sparkled whenever he saw her. She thought of his lips, his full pink lips, wet from kissing her with a new love he hadn't wanted.

"Oh Luka, my beautiful, golden, haired angel."

She whispered regretfully, followed by a lamenting sigh. It was too late. She'd slept with Kaine. No turning to Luka in the future. She'd made her choice, and sent Luka to London. She was a big girl and finally on her own.

Holly descended the staircase with remorseful thoughts of Luka crowding her thoughts. However, she sensed somewhere in the dark castle — Kaine awaited her arrival. She stood quietly, listening for the slightest footfall. Where was he? Did Kaine no longer care? Had his love died with her confession as quickly as the flame in the gutted candle? That brought a tight pinch to her heart from that awful thought. She dismissed it and the cold hardness of the stone floor beneath her freezing feet was all too familiar.

Holly pushed further. She couldn't hear the echoes of her own steps, so aware the castle was silent — but not empty. The ghosts of centuries past whispered to her, guiding her. She felt the chilling sensation of being listened for … something waited for her. With each step, her panic raced.

Where are you, Kaine? Why won't you come back for me?

Hadn't their lovemaking been sweet enough?

Rough enough?

Violent enough?

Passionate enough?

It had been perfect for her.

Dark, shapeless forms leaped out toward Holly from all angles. She passed a large, cracked antique mirror on the wall. The lightning flashed and she caught a glimpse of her ragged reflection, dark and distorted, frightening her, as in a house of mirrors in the freak shows. Burning tears sprang into her eyes, quickly welling up, and then spilling down her cheeks.

"Where the hell are you Kaine?" she cried aloud into the maze of inky darkness as she cautiously wandered around too many dark rooms until they all became the same. She started to consider she might be walking in one giant circle.

Then, something flickered.

Was that a quivering light she saw at the end of this corridor?

Or her imagination?

Her heart pounded in her ears with a new hope. A cold, brittle air blasted against her warm cheeks stinging them. When she arrived at the doorway, she discovered the recording studio. The door opened wider as if a dark mouth waiting to devour her. She stepped in and pushed the door a bit more to close it with the heel of her foot.

The first thing she saw behind the massive recording console was the Hard Rock video "Now That I've Found You" playing on the screen with the sound conspicuously missing. She stared at a blatant reminder of a better time with Kaine as the frames slowed one-by-one. She watched their incredible kiss. Their lips touch. The last of her madness drained and her heartbeat quieted. A sharp rumble of thunder made her gasp, and suddenly the images on the screen disappeared.

"Do you see how much I loved you?"

The ominous voice questioned, puncturing the darkened room.

Holly didn't move a muscle or flick an eye, as the inky blackness of the room worked to unnerve her, affixing her to the spot.

"Don't be frightened. The lightning has blown the electricity. Soon, the backup generators will come on and then the heat." The subdued voice reassured.

Holly waited and then spoke into the darkness.

"Kaine? Where are you?"

"I'm somewhere back in time trying to recapture the moment when I was totally happy. The moment I fell in love with you."

She hung her head. Her chin dragged her chest. She squeezed her eyes shut and sent a quick thought of thanks. He still loved her, though the resolve in his voice was saying he wasn't pleased.

There is a limit with Luka — she quickly remembered.

Kaine spoke softly, his words wrapped in a profound weariness.

"What is it you want me to do to prove myself worthy, My Lady? Do you want me to slay dragons? Do you want kingdoms? Do you want jewels? I can buy you the moon and the stars. My accountant says I have enough money. What is it I can do to wipe Luka's unfettered spell from your thoughts? How can I erase the pleasure you enjoy when he touches your body? Please, tell me, My Lady," as his voice faded on the last few words.

Holly shook her head. She didn't want to hear those ugly words and they shook her from her trance. "Kaine, Luka, is not my destiny!"

"I wish it were that simple. It's not anymore. You may believe your words to be true. But you're part of Luka now. I know, because I see you in his eyes. He will not set you free, at least, not to come to me. Tis a pity because I am alone again, only it will be worse because I have had a few days of happiness with you," he claimed as his voice hovered on the edge of despair.

"Kaine, please ... forget what I said to you. You ... you made me so mad, I said the first thing that popped into my head to stop you."

"You have succeeded."

"You surely can't believe this distance is what I want?"

"You said what was on your mind," Kaine declared as he struck a match, and the darkness disappeared. His beautiful face had lost its glow. It remained expressionless, blank, his eyes empty.

She hated this distance growing quickly between them like fire in dry leaves.

"It seems the generators are not going to work, after all." He submitted as motionless as the expression on his face. He turned the high back swivel chair away from her and vanished. A tiny, yellow lance of fire from a match tip radiated, casting a dim glow.

The faint hue became her other companion in the darkness. The flash of another flame caused the head of his shadow to project onto the wall and dance manically. Kaine's hand came into her line of vision. He sat a thick, white, pillar candle on the console, and its light danced frantically. He spun the swivel chair around to face her coming into full view.

A bar of bright, golden light dropped the ragged edges of his silhouette onto the cobblestone floor while the angled saffron light kissed the length of his naked body. Half draped in a rich, royal blue, tapestry, Kaine sat, one leg crossed over the other. His long, chestnut brown hair hung like a royal cape fanned about his shoulders. The lord of the castle was in, and Kaine Walker was breath-stealing, knee bending beautiful.

It was then the time-traveler spoke.

"Why don't you tell me, luv? What is it you do want? Maybe it would be easier to start there." Kaine ventured to persuade her to speak while staring straight into her eyes. It was impossible to miss the slight edge of contempt still riding the tone of his voice. Clearly, he was not used to his point-of-view challenged.

Holly didn't know what to say. A barrage of ugly emotions arrived. She didn't know all their names. All the while hot, stinging tears were blurring her vision. She took a deep breath and reined in every impulse to run and throw her arms around Kaine and kiss his sweet lips.

Instead, she retained her dignity.

She moved in soundlessly. She passed the doorway to slip up on a stool. She flung her long, damp, braid behind her and tried to stop shivering. Not from the cool temperature of the castle because the heat had stopped but because of being dangerously close to the chilling edge of losing Kaine, long before they'd had a chance to let their love flourish.

"I don't know where to begin." She ventured in a shaken voice, hesitant to look into his eyes and find nothing. She glanced in his direction and slightly shook her head in disbelief.

His poker face revealed no emotions as he pulled a large bottle of orange juice from the black edges of the candlelight. Kaine wrapped his lips around the top of the bottle, and sucked in a giant swig, swallowed easily and then set the bottle between his crossed legs. He took in a deep, patient breath and invited her.

"Why don't you start at the beginning...."

Chapter Nineteen

FELL ON BLACK DAYS

Beginning. How many words would it take this time? All she knew for sure, the time had arrived to explain her past to him while she had Kaine without interruption.

It was dangerous, the last thing she needed to do was to confuse issues and gain his pity with the tragic tale she'd kept secret. She was ready to share because her future depended on his understanding.

Holly hesitantly started her story.

"I met a remarkable man ... seems like many lifetimes ago. He was where I'm from in Santa Barbara, California. Sounds silly, I met Jon De La Guerra in preschool. By the time, we were ten he had a pair of dreamy, blue, eyes that were hard to ignore. He was always tan, taller than I was thin, well-built and showed early signs of becoming a handsome man. His hair was long, dark, cut one length as the surfers in town wore in those days. I followed him everywhere.

"He lived near East Beach, in a comfortable house with a

Spanish tiled roof, near the Milpas area. His dad was the black sheep from old money, the De La Guerras. They even had a street named after them. Anyway, his dad's love of flying drew him to work at the Santa Barbara airport because he loved to repair airplane engines. To add insult to injury, his dad flew privately for the rich and famous in town. Which in his case were his wealthy families' friends and that upset Jon's grandfather.

"Jon lived a simple life away from the De La Guerra money. I remember his fingernails were always full of grease from working beside his dad on the plane engines. It was a given he would become a pilot although the De La Guerra's had different aspirations for their only male grandchild.

"At the same time, there was another extraordinarily important person in my life, Brett." She stopped to take another deep breath. "Brett Templeton was always tall for his age, blond-haired and blue-eyed, unbelievably good-looking."

Kaine uncrossed his legs and shook them as if they were asleep. He blurted out if he finally realized something important. "Are you talking about Brett Templeton? The solicitor that defended Mason Collins' in his murder trial, in L.A.?"

"The same."

"Fuck, Holly. Fuck! ... so when you were speaking of Brett, all this time, you've been telling me, you're engaged to THE fucking Brett Templeton? He'll send every blood sucking solicitor he knows, to sue me as revenge for stealing you away!"

His face shined brightly, and the gleam in his eyes was surprising.

"My ... Lady, you're, so full of surprises. Please, go on," he encouraged as a tiny smug smile threatened to grace the corner of his lips.

Great!

He'd said — *stealing her away.*

She was still his lady.

He was back.

She needed to hold his interest, so she continued.

"The same one — and though we are engaged, I'm not going to marry him." She decided to throw in to smooth the waters.

"Remember, I have a loving boyfriend."

Kaine smiled appreciably.

Relieved and happy, she continued.

"Brett's parents routinely hired Jon's dad to fly them about locally. Jon and Brett, the same age, played together all of their childhood. Brett and Jon were counterparts — one fair, the other dark. Jon was so adorable that Brett's mother took pity on the motherless boy and fell in love with him, as we all did. Like you and Luka, they became as close as any two brothers can be."

"Who told you that?" Kaine barked wearing an expression of puzzlement at how she had learned something as intimate as his relationship with Luka.

"Lilly. She mentioned you and Luka had been together a long time and were like brothers."

"Some back-stabbing brother Luka turned out to be," Kaine confirmed with a grunt, looking away from her.

"There are good things about being brothers. Jon and Brett had the best, and they fought with each other too and protected each other. And according to Jon, fell in love with the same girl."

"I see this situation is not new to you, My Lady. Please continue so I may know what Brett did to win you away from Jon."

His question, so easy to ask, the answer would take so many words to explain. There would be many joyful and devastating emotions to go through to make him understand. The question was, could she make it through without going into the madness again?

"True, the story is similar. Like you, I only had eyes for Jon De La Guerra." She paused to picture his sweet face in her mind. Under her breath, she expressed her true sentiments.

"My Jon."

But Kaine heard her. He reacted forcefully, his voice loud, blasting her.

"Your Jon? If you're in love with someone else Holly, we can stop the story right now, and I will become nothing more than a bittersweet memory."

Kaine's biting words took strength to fight. She knew his stinging words resulted from the threat he thought existed and didn't understand. She was wandering out into deep waters, and she needed to explain the story quicker. She headed straight for the point.

"I will always love Jon. But things have changed. I love you a different love ... a woman's love. Please, give me one chance to explain." She pleaded softly.

Apparently satisfied with her explanation, Kaine settled back, pulling the bottle of orange juice to his puckered lips.

She watched the honey-colored liquid drip from the side of

his mouth. Holly stopped every wild urge to run to him, lick the nectar from his delicious lips, and simply work her way down to the tip of his scrumptious hard love. She momentarily thought of how much she had enjoyed loving him in the tub, and the moistness happened instantly, as she crossed her legs. Kaine quickly replaced her, wiping the escaping drops with the back of his hand — effective, but not nearly as much fun as she was thinking.

She shook her head for a second to regain her thoughts.

"Jon's father became alcoholic as his war memories haunted and destroyed his life. He turned gray before his time and being a gentle, loving man, let Jon drift closer to my family and me. I too am an only child. My dad, Arthur Hill, is the editor of the local newspaper, and mom, Anne Hill, happily stayed at home loving and taking care of all our needs. Before too long Jon had the guest room filled with his personal things. He seldom went to see his father and my house became home to him.

"Meanwhile, Brett was the third cog in this wheel. He went everywhere with us, all each other's best friend. Brett's great looks meant he had a new girlfriend every week. Some from old money, new money, no money — he didn't care. Being rich also meant Brett attended the finest private school in Santa Barbara.

"When we were ready for the university, Brett's dad had his future mapped out. However, Brett was able to fight his litigating dad and attend a local university right out of prep school. As I recall, he threatened to run away with a rock band if they tried to send him back east."

She smiled at the irony of that thought.

"Brett stayed home with Jon and me and played big man on campus. All the girls naturally flocked to him. He always said he envied us. That Jon had the only girl he truly loved and was looking for a girl like me."

"It seems I am not alone. Many men think you're perfect for them." Kaine pointed out, his voice a bit apologetic. It would appear he might be becoming more reasonable.

"Kaine, I assure you, it wasn't me he was in love with, but the idea of me, the steady girl, always there. That took more work than he was willing to give. What Jon, and I, had together was for the young, innocent, and, so unique. I cherished every day I spent with him. Not many people can find that special love."

"I had...." Kaine's said, his words meant to be sweet, targeted Holly's guilt, and she heard the words as harsh and condemning.

What she put forth was. "And you, and I, *have*. That's why what I have to tell you is, so personally important to us. Please don't drift from me. I'm trying to explain in my own way, what has happened to bring me to you."

He leaned back, his body language saying he would give her a chance. He stared at her, waiting, listening. She needed to find the courage to go back into time.

"One night we were dipping into an old past time of ours, as odd as it sounds, blowing up pipe bombs on deserted stretches of the beach — been doing it for years. However, this night we weren't alone. When the bomb went off, we ran up on the bluff and right into a vicious gang. These guys were hard, menacing, and carried weapons.

"Jon and Brett were wearing were shorts, T-shirts, and their long hair well below their shoulders, blowing from the gentle sea breeze. The gang members taunted Jon and Brett about their hair, outnumbering them two-to-one. Moments later, they punched Jon and Brett in the face. When the thrill waned, they turned their brutal attention to me. They... tore off my clothing and held me down, making it impossible to escape."

Holly tried to stop the flow of the ugly memories, reliving each segment of the savage attack. She took a few deep breaths, to keep her tears from leaking like a broken faucet.

"The stench of the liquor and the hate in their eyes scared me badly. I screamed and screamed. I'll never forget the filthy hand that clamped over my mouth. I could barely breathe. I listened to the muffled sounds of bodies beaten. My virginal fear escalated, knowing if Jon and Brett, could not break free, this monster was going to rape me. Then he would undoubtedly pass me around to his friends, and then possibly kill me."

She dragged in another breath, wondering how she ended up on this dark path five thousand miles away in an English castle.

"I'm so sorry, sweetheart. I wish I could have been there to protect you." Kaine consoled tenderly.

She couldn't look him in the eyes, not just yet. By the sound of his voice, she didn't want to know what pity looked like planted in his eyes.

"You're, sweet to say that. Nevertheless, everything happened, so fast, and so slow. We all heard an explosion, precious moments before this hideous creature penetrated me. Mercifully, he stopped and groped for his pants as he ran off into the darkness, followed by the rest of the menacing gang.

One pipe bomb faltered as they often did and didn't go off on time. The explosion scared those horrible creatures, assuming we might not be alone.

"It took a lot of Tequila that night to calm our fears, anger, and ease the pain of our bloodied bodies. Somewhere in the blur of long time respect, and friendship, Jon made Brett promise and swear to him that if anything ever happened to him, Brett would take care of me.

"Understand, our motivation was from gratefulness to be alive. We performed the old time childhood game of pricking our fingers to draw blood. We wanted to become as close as we possibly could, blood brothers and blood sister. We would be together always — ah, the hopes and philosophies of youth. How could we have known?"

"I understand, this childhood ritual is the origin of the obligation Brett expects you to fulfill?" Kaine asked as if surprised.

"I believe so. I need to make you understand why he decided to honor the oath of obligation."

"I do, to fulfill the promise — something had to happen to Jon. Is this what scars your heart and mind?"

Kaine's voice was satiny, smooth, the voice of the man she'd fallen in love with so quickly.

"I believe that." In fact, Holly knew damn well it was why.

"A woman with your sense of duty is rare in my world. It is an honor to love you, My Lady. As for Brett? I have no reply. He assumes he has won you from Jon. Let the best chap win."

Holly hung her head, knowing how a prized horse felt at the auction.

"That's not how it is, Brett hasn't won. That was not the

end of the story. It is traumatic Kaine, as the scars on your back. However, you don't wish to share with me the origin of that pain. Sometimes secrets are more dangerous when left to grow and fester, keeping us alone, afraid to trust anyone. You're correct, my scars are many, and also deep. The only difference between us is I'm willing to share my secrets."

Her words seemed to reach him, and Kaine predicted. "One day, I promise, I will tell you about the scars I bear that you can see. Maybe on another day, I will tell you about the scars you can't see. For now, I am intrigued and want to know what has happened to Jon?"

Kaine's mood changed. His words were positive, more hopeful, and he was regaining his balance with her.

She could even see a bit of the old light flickering in his eyes, and he had promised her another day. Holly released a small oath of thanks — more days with Kaine.

"Brett, Jon, and I, believed in the magic incantation practiced that night. As we grew older, and after high school, our attentions turn to careers. Brett and I already loved laws and rules. We remembered the vow, promising we would be the keepers of the ancient law of the blood-brother/sister ritual. Or, so we believed.

"Brett had a strong mischievous streak too, and loved the breaking of laws, whereas, I stood fast, wanting to preserve the law. Jon lived between his love of journalism that took him to the center of what was shaping our world, and his love of flying into the solitary peace only he knew existed.

"To Brett's and my delight, his growing love for the law. It wasn't a surprise. Night after night, Jon would join in our heated debates on justice and the legal process, and learned he would make a remarkable lawyer. Soon the collective dream was our own office, Templeton, Hill, and De La Guerra. That was where I lived, in the middle of these two men.

"Living in the middle of two men is a place you're familiar with, only now it's Luka and me."

"Not familiar! There're many differences, one being Brett didn't have any romantic interest in me. There had been a woman, one he'd planned to be his loving wife. They had their own tragedy befall them and since then, Brett's never mentioned her name. I don't think he's ever come to terms with her betrayal.

"For the next few months, he slept with any woman that came for him and the line never ended. He drank heavily and swallowed pills. It was as if he was trying to kill himself to stop his misery. Jon and I couldn't reach him. No one could ... until ..."

Holly paused. "Well, I'm in a hurry now. I must slow down."

Holly twisted on the stool, wondering where she would find the strength for the next leg of her story.

She stood and walked closer to Kaine, reached down for the orange juice bottle and gratefully drained a long swallow. She handed it back to him while the smooth juice lined her throat all the way to her stomach.

By the time she crossed back to her perch, her belly had warmed, leaving only her heart to ache.

"My Lady Love?"

"I'm okay. I need a little space to tell the rest of this."

Her body was warming a bit, but her heart still ached. The old painful feelings were returned slamming into her harder than she would have imagined. The demons were joyfully stabbing her repeatedly, punishing her for remembering, making her want to run.

Holly looked up to find Kaine sitting so still, watching her. To calm herself she grabbed a breath of courage and confided.

"I've never been able to tell anyone what I'm about to tell you."

Chapter Twenty

DON'T FEAR THE REAPER

She pushed on. "My dear, sweet Jon." Holly ignored the pain surging through her heart. "It's been a long time if ever, that a man's attention made me see myself as truly special."

"I am sorry I have failed you." He apologized. His voice was defensive and rigid. His eyes had forgotten to hide his pain as he threw her a hurtful glance.

"Please, let me explain, and try not to get upset, because at first, you're not going to like what I have to say. Wait, it will get better.

"It's not that you haven't made me feel special. It's, well, the always beautiful and charming Luka, met me first. He came out of nowhere like a warm summer breeze and caught me off guard, with his lavish attention. It took an impressive man like him to blow me out of my private Hell. When I was set free, I discovered a brand new world. When I looked around, the first wondrous man I saw — was you.

"Like you, I've kept to myself these last seven years. I've

dated a few of Brett's friends over the years, no one worth mentioning and never long enough to have a physical relationship with because no one ever paid me any attention until Luka. No one ever saw me beyond Brett's shadow, a broken, shy, woman. You see, I do understand what you were trying to tell me in the hotel, about being loved for yourself."

Kaine's voice was cool and unyielding. "What do Jon and Brett have to do with Luka?"

"I'm getting to that."

I hope.

She encouraged herself, not having any idea where she was heading — except into Hell.

"Earlier you mentioned Brett fighting dragons. I realized you were kidding about the dragons to keep the fantasy going. When I finish my story, you will see how Brett and I are tied together out of obligation or duty. Call it what you like, but it's not from passion or romantic love. He does not try to slay dragons for me. He is too busy slaying them for him to make a name for himself.

"Now you see how I became invisible. I was the proper choice, a given to become Brett's wife. Fortunately, at the time, he was willing to take me along with him. Given the situation, I would never have had a life of my own because it would always be the life he had provided, his dream. We could have been a great defense team in L.A., only he had conveniently kept me busy with pre-trial motions, investigating leads, and rumors, so I never took the bar exam. Well, no more!"

The words rang true. In that split second, Holly allowed a closer level of security with Kaine — time to tell him the truth, the whole truth, and nothing but the truth.

Kaine interrupted her thought. "Am I correct to assume you worked with the defense team for the Collins' murder case?"

"Yes, the core defense team." She volunteered a bit over sensitive.

"Are you the lady that sat behind Brett with the dark hair? I watched more of the trial than I'd like to admit on the satellite dish. They always showed a woman he would arrive, and depart with, but I would never have put it together that you're *that* lady?"

"The dark hair — this color is a red rinse. We are a pair aren't we Kaine? Each familiar with the others' lives, and now, beginning to discover our true selves, the face behind the mask.

"You can see, with Brett, I would never be able to practice criminal law, the kind I wanted. I would be the wife, his prop or ornament, whatever you choose to call my position. Brett is one hundred and ten percent ambition. He will eventually run for public office. Everyone's already talking about Congress. He's being groomed as we speak.

"I hope you can understand why you made me, so angry when you said, Luka knew better than to touch what was yours. Once again, I felt like a piece of property. That no one was seeing me. I had vanished. Coming from you, it hurt Kaine. It cut deep because I thought you were the one person that could understand what it was like to be invisible, living behind your rock star shield."

He sat silently.

She could barely make out his facial features as he slugged back a short swig from the bottle.

His voice pierced the darkness.

"Continue..."

"Yes, I must tell you the rest of the story before I lose my courage." Tiny drops fell from her eyes. She caught them with a finger on her cheeks. She wasn't sure it would be possible to tell Kaine. "I've never been able to use words to tell anyone what I'm about to share with you."

After a string of long quiet seconds, Kaine softly spoke to her. "It is okay, my love, you don't have to tell me any more. I can see how it's upsetting you, maybe, another time."

"Thank you, but there has to be a time, and it may as well be tonight. I've come this far, and it's too important to our future. I don't want to lose you simply because I couldn't bear to tell you tonight."

His voice became, soft, sweet, reminding her heart, he loved her too, and he confessed. "I'm here, for good or bad, it won't be easy for you to lose me. Tell me My Lady Love. What is your tale of woe? What happened to you?"

She sat, knocked out by his words, so loving, creating a safe place where she could confide in him.

For good or bad.

A breath quickly rose to help summon her courage then she blurted out.

"I was three months pregnant with Jon's child."

Kaine interrupted, "I want children. If you have a child...."

Holly cut him off, "Thank you that is so sweet. But no, that's not it Kaine. Please, let me tell you my way." She took another breath and continued. "We were deliriously happy. We'd arranged to finish at the university, and go on to law school. His becoming a father had been the final push for Jon to decide to become a lawyer, responsibilities, and all. We announced our plans to be married when we knew I was with child. We'd decided to keep the pregnancy a secret, and my parents helped plan our wedding. Brett was our only confidant, and the two doted on me like mother hens.

"The day of the wedding a storm blew in, a surprise to everyone. We'd expected light rain. Instead, it turned into one of the worst storms of the century. Jon got a call and came to see me before the wedding. I still can't remember what I said to him. Something like, 'No, Jon you can't see me now. It's bad luck.'" Holly stopped. She could hardly speak, and her bottom lip wouldn't stop quivering.

"Sweetheart, you don't have to tell me. I can see this is tearing you up." Kaine spoke, so softly.

She looked up and saw the sympathy on his face — his pity.

"No ... I will tell you." She remembered where she had left off in her story. How could she have known what was going to happen? If only she'd stopped him.

"Jon said, 'It's Dad. He's due back with a private party. It's close to time for him to stand up for me. He wouldn't miss this. But his plane hasn't radioed in, and I'm worried.'

"We agreed to wait as long as possible to be married. In the end, the ceremony was not the one I'd dreamed of because of the storm beat against the church walls, threatening to break the vows we had taken. Jon was dreadfully upset because his father wasn't present.

"When we reached the end of the aisle as man and wife, Jon turned to me and said, 'You know I love you more than life its self. ...I have to go and look for Dad. You and my son sit and wait. I'll be back when I can.'

"Jon kissed me fiercely. As if he knew something, he wasn't telling me. I overheard him tell Brett, 'Look after her while I'm gone. I'm counting on you."

"Brett said, 'Always, Jon. You can always count on me brother, Holly's safe with me.'

"The words we chose, so cryptic, our souls saying goodbye.

"No one is sure what happened. Jon's Cessna plane was missing. He'd filed no flight plan. Jon had flown those skies more than he had walked on the ground." Holly fought every urge, not to break down, and sob. The deep pain was gushing and was worse than she'd ever imagined. Seven years had not been long enough. She took a short, ragged breath and pushed on in spite of the horrible memory lashing her mind.

"I stayed at the Templeton mansion. Brett threw us a magnificent wedding reception as our wedding gift. Hell of a reception, the bride in constant tears, and the guests sat about with sunken faces. It was late when the news arrived, and Brett came to me.

"Brett looked worse than the night he'd been beaten up by the gang. His voice was so soft. I almost didn't hear his words as he spoke. 'Jon's dad landed. Everyone on the plane is safe, just shaken by the storm.'

"Brett came closer. I watched tears well in his eyes. I didn't want to listen to him. I'm not sure I ever have. It was something inside me that heard his words, oh not in my mind, not the place between my ears, but somewhere deeper.

"'Jon's.... Dead.... A wing of his plane was found on one of the Channel Islands. The rest of the plane went ... with him ... into the ocean during the storm.'

"I felt nothing. A few seconds later, a cold chill, ripple from my ankles to my scalp. The cold flurry continued mercifully, freezing my feelings, and I can remember wondering how long the coolness would last. The idea was impossible to believe. That Jon would never return. He would never see the son he was sure I was carrying, born and grow into a brilliant man as his father. I would never kiss his sweet lips again." Holly's tears of mourning washed over her like a tidal wave.

Kaine sat still. Then he quietly summoned.

"Come to me, My Lady. Let me comfort you."

"No," she managed to say. "No, please allow me to finish. Or, you will never know why I am so afraid of losing you."

"You will never lose me," Kaine assured with conviction.

Holly wiped away her falling tears and looked at him to let him know she had heard his loving words. She grabbed a solitary breath.

"That night I stayed at the Templeton mansion against my parent's wishes. I couldn't face going home where Jon and I had lived together for the majority of our childhood. Brett set me up in an exquisite bedroom down the hall from him. I was given a mild sedative because of my pregnancy."

She stopped, pushed her head back, and took another breath. She glanced around the room to find it silent and dimly lit. She saw Kaine waiting for her to tell him what tormented her. His eyes showed her, his heart about to break because of her suffering. She hoped that wasn't pity surfacing in his eyes. She wanted that look to be his love. She needed his love, not pity. She was finished with pity.

A sudden flash of second thoughts made her wonder if she

wanted to give up her demons that tortured her daily. Would she know who she was if she didn't have those dark forces to pick at her with the 'what ifs' that had driven her to madness?

Holly paused, took another breath while pondering if she could continue then relaxed and feasted on the magnificence of Kaine.

Yes, his love was worth any agony.

"It was about two in the morning when I woke up with terrible abdominal cramps. They grew worse by the minute. I was barely able to drag myself to the bathroom before I found blood seeping down from under my wedding gown. I'd wish I'd listen to my mother, and taken it off, but it had been the last thing Jon had touched when he'd kissed me. I could smell him on the gown.

"When I lifted it, I saw the red, streaming down my legs. I leaned against the basin. The cramping was too much, and it was coming so fast. I cried out for help, but I was in the back of the mansion. It didn't take long for me to realize I had a miscarriage. I lost the last of Jon. I would be left with nothing but memories. Then one gut-wrenching contraction dragged me to the floor, and the last link to Jon passed. I laid on the cold floor despondent. I don't know for how long. At some point, I'd made the decision." She looked up to Kaine. He sat mesmerized by each of her words.

"...I'd decided to join my baby and his father. ...I'd found a razor for overnight guests in a drawer. And Kaine, you'd be surprised to learn it didn't hurt at all. Nothing compared to the pain I was experiencing.

"I lay waiting for a merciful death. Before I closed my eyes, I caught a flash of Jon in the doorway. He was holding our baby wrapped in a blue blanket coming for me ... calling me to come and care for them ... love them."

She quickly looked away from Kaine. Her tears burned her eyes, but no more than the memory of love shattering in her chest. Her stomach twisted into knots. She made a fist with her hand and placed it over her mouth. The devastating memory was worse than she would have imagined. She clammed up a bit, wiping her tears away, then found another breath, and continued onward.

"It's not like they say about leaving a note. There hadn't been any thought of locating a pen or notepaper. No time, I was leaving, on my way to join my husband, and child, my family....

"But it was not to be. Brett found me before I could. Said Jon had come to him in a dream and told him to check in on me. Said, he woke up so quickly, he'd run down the hallway stark naked.

"Somehow, I'd had the presence of mind to lock the door. But Brett broke it down, and it couldn't have been a pleasant sight for him. My blood splattered everywhere and all over my beautiful white, wedding dress. I woke up in the hospital four days later with my wrists taped. I missed Jon's memorial service and later I was referred to a health spa — the polite term for sanitarium or a loony bin in those days. While I was there, I reclaimed my maiden name. It was too painful to be called Mrs. De La Guerra.

"My mind was bent, my spirit crushed. It took seven months to walk out of that place. Brett, bless his heart, was there whenever I needed him. He cursed himself for leaving me alone that night. Said, he should have slept on the couch in the guest room with me. That was the beginning of Brett's new purpose in life — to watch over me.

"He made me promise to never hurt myself again because that would break his promise to Jon. And he couldn't bear that. Brett only knew one way to watch me. He encouraged me to finish my university courses, and then I went on to law school with him. However, he took the exam and I didn't. I wasn't strong enough at the time. We both moved to L.A. He'd arrange to keep me close by making sure I was hired at his father's firm in Beverly Hills, as a paralegal and investigator. Or, shall we say wife-in-training. He has kept me involved with high profile and sensational criminal trials that Los Angeles can provide. Still, I was alone and, so was he. We were all we had."

"Brett Templeton is a true friend Holly. You have been truly lucky to have him." Kaine affirmed with admiration shining in his bright blue eyes.

"I see you do understand how we are tied together. After seven years, Brett thought it was the time to marry. You and I know he will always love the other woman whether she deserves it or not. Ours would not have been a loveless marriage because I do love Brett, but we have never been in romantic love with each other. I thought at the time of his proposal I would only love Jon ... that was true until I kissed you.

"Brett waits in L.A., for me to decide when we will be married. Instead, I am in England, totally in love with you, my Precious One."

"I am, so sorry, My Lady Love." Kaine sympathized, his apology direct, and sincere.

Holly sat up straight. Her eyes flamed with disgust, as she defiantly vented, "I don't want your pity! Everyone reacts the same way ... sad eyes, so apologetic, so full of pity. I didn't see that in your eyes after you kissed me at the Hard Rock, or in front of Buckingham Palace, or at your hotel, here in the castle today, or this evening. I didn't see the word ... *widow* in your eyes. It's such an ugly word. It means that out of the blue you've been left, abandoned due to a horrible twist of fate, and you're alone with no plans for the future. That's what I see in your eyes now, your damn pity."

"You're, so wrong my sweet, Lady Love." Kaine corrected with a quiet even-toned voice. "What you see is my admiration, and respect for a brave lady, a loving lady who sacrificed herself and submitted to the unbearable pain of her past to prove you love me. And you're right. I heard you. I am self-centered, selfish and a brat, still ... I've been called worse. I've experienced much pain myself, some similar to yours, but some of the sufferings you have endured, I can't imagine. I'd have done anything to spare you. But...."

"But what?"

What else was there to say?

"I understand your loyalty to Brett's career and reputation. The obligation you hold for each other. It will be hard for you to tell Brett about me if he hasn't already read about us in the papers. I understand how you're being linked to a rock star could affect his aspirations to run for Congress. It will certainly make for sensational headlines.

"I sincerely apologize for my lousy behavior upstairs. I am a stupid, stupid fool. My only defense is I love you too. This love is new, intense, and my jealousy won. It was a ghastly way to behave. I even surprised myself. But the thought of you with others, especially Luka, well, I may be a fool, but human, as well. Sometimes, too human. And, I understand your devotion to Jon's memory, your loyalties to Brett ... now, tell me about Luka."

"Luka? Why do you persist in bringing up Luka?"

"Because, I finally understand that he is the only one that can destroy our future."

Chapter Twenty-One

BED OF ROSES

If she could only tell Kaine about Luka.

"I am going to tell you the complete truth because I don't want any secrets or confusion. I'm sorry to begin with these feeble words, but I honestly don't know how to explain what is between Luka and me.

"I'd guess, like you, everyone needs to be seen as their selves. Luka happened to be the first man to see me there on the London street. Jon had been a boy lost in puppy love and then grew to be a young man lost in the throes of a young man's dream of a wife and family.

"Luka is a full-grown man, with a sophisticated man's expectations and needs. Plus, he is, so terribly handsome, and charming. He was also kind, thoughtful, and attentive those first few hours I arrived in London. If it hadn't been for Luka, I would have never been beautiful for the Hard Rock shoot. Remember, you didn't even recognize me as the plain girl backstage with Luka."

"But I told you then, I wanted to kiss that girl, you, that

night, to take you away from Luka." His voice softly reminded.

"Yes, but you told me at the Hard Rock, how different I was, a new creation of Luka's. I would never have had the confidence to think I was beautiful enough to attract your attention.

"I am sorry," Holly, insisted but added, "believe me when I say you're my Precious One. How do I explain? Luka's, so ... overwhelming. Don't think I'm blind or stupid. I can see he adores me. Coming from Luka, it's — wonderful. And if you're going to hate me because I do feel affection for Luka, then I want you to walk away understanding one thing. Somehow, Luka recognized I needed help. He offered attention, companionship and maybe understood how much I needed love. It is not lost on me to question if it is me Luka truly sees, and not a faded illusion of his long lost Carrin.

"As for me? He didn't care if I was Brett's shadow, or the Holly Hill, whose friends, and family think needs to be watched. I'm almost twenty-nine years old Kaine, and Luka was the first man that ever allowed me to grow up, and become a woman, and that was amazing. He did not try to sleep with me, all the same, I will admit to you, so there are no secrets between us about Luka. I was so disappointed."

She couldn't look into Kaine's eyes.

Not now.

"Luka saw me. He saw that I deeply wanted to be beautiful for a man. Without him, my dream would never have come true. Jon was the only other man that looked at me the way Luka did, the only man that let me play and tease him. Not since Jon has a man given me the space to experiment with my charms. I wanted to use them to win my lover's heart. Only, surprise! It turned out Luka wasn't to be my lover; my lover is you, Kaine."

He shrugged his shoulders. "But you had won me from the beginning."

"Forgive me, as you would say, I'm only human. I didn't know, and Luka is, so flesh-and-blood. It seems he instinctively knew how to bring out a side of me, I'd never known existed. I will acknowledge that I have a difficult time controlling myself when I am around him.

"But he doesn't matter Kaine, you're everything I've ever wanted and dreamed of in a man, sensitive, creative, and a fantastic lover. If I had not met you, I would confess. It's true. I'd be in love with Luka. What's not to love? But Luka has one fatal flaw ... you. As ridiculous as it sounds because it has been less than three days, I did not fall in love with Luka as I have with you. Do you hear me, Kaine Walker?"

Silence.

The light reflected off the neck of the bottle half-filled with orange juice that Kaine moved in the shadows.

"Kaine, this whole situation is so unbelievable. Look around, I've become a princess in a far off land, and I have two handsome princes fighting for me."

Nothing but crushing silence.

Predictably, Kaine didn't want to hear what she'd have to say about Luka. She stumbled on, not knowing where she would end this tale.

"I don't have to remind you of Luka abilities. He possesses the skills of a five-star general behind the scenes. However, I do have concerns about him since he works for you. That because he has attempted to build a relationship with me, has displeased you. I can only hope you won't be hard on him. Please remember that it was Luka that made me believe I could attract your attention, and keep your interest, and I owe Luka more that he'll ever know."

With that admission, Kaine sprang up from his chair. The antique tapestry fell to the floor as he hit the console with his fist, and bellowed.

"Don't you understand? I don't want you to come to me from Luka. I want you to feel beautiful and desirable because you see it *first* in *my* eyes — not his!" He shouted, pounding on his chest when he'd said *'first'* and *'my.'*

"Look, Holly, Luka is not who, or what you think. There is a lot you need to know. For now, I will give you a quick *Hurrikaine* history lesson. It's essential I get you up to speed."

Holly leaned against the wall thankful he was about to open up, realizing he had dropped the castle fantasy dialog. As usual, his words couldn't have surprised her more.

Kaine took a quick swig of orange juice, seeming to mellow out from his outburst. He sat back down, and then crossed his legs on the chair. He placed the juice bottle back into the hollow of his legs, and then quietly spoke.

"I know you believe you are fair, counselor, and I love your spunky spirit and sense of conscience. I do understand much more than you think about the painful events in your life. I've had a few tragedies too, but that is not what you need to know tonight. What's important is, for you, and me, to find a united front, to keep our love from being torn apart. Remember, I have lived a life that most would champion, others would be ashamed of, but during all my years with the band, Luka has been beside me.

"Luka booked the band's gigs. The jobs got bigger and so did the money. We made a few dollars, then hundreds of dollars, then thousands, then tens of thousands, then millions and ultimately, hundreds of millions of dollars together. Until I met you, I would truthfully have to say, Luka Hunter was the best, damned thing that ever happened to me."

"Are you saying you love Luka?" she asked cautiously.

"Sounds cliché, but I do. He's my brother. But, I can hate him too, as strongly, and more than I ever thought possible these past two days. The intensity even alarms me. When we were close, we were two-of-a-kind. We have shared more women than you would possibly think. We have swapped them, played horrible games with them, and slept with them in the same bed simultaneously. Does that shock you? Women have fought each other over *us* since the beginning, but we didn't care. This is the first time we fight each other for a woman ... and her love. You ... My Lady Love, you.

"Please beware. Beside Luka's obvious good looks and charm, he is sharp and cunning. I have never seen Luka lose anything he went after, My Lady. So, don't fool yourself into thinking he has gracefully bowed out, and given you up to me without one hell of a fight. Not Luka. He has not given up the pursuit. He is merely amused. My involvement sweetens the stakes."

"You sound, so arrogant and make me sound like a grand prize."

"My apologies, I don't mean that. Understand, this situation with Luka will get much worse before it gets better. After Paris, Luka will leave the tour and return to L.A. This brings up the obvious problem with you, and Luka, living in the same town while I'm trapped on an eighteen-month world tour. Don't ever underestimate him. He's counting on the fact that while I'm away, he has access to you. He's expecting to win you with his strong influence over you. And I can't think about that now, or I'd go mental. When Luka leaves the tour, it will be the end of an incredibly long partnership."

Holly's mind worked overtime while he unfolded his story. His prediction appeared valid. Plans were made from the beginning to meet in L.A.

Show me the fun places.

A thousand sunsets.

Yes, Luka had plans for her. Kaine's keen observations made it clear he knew exactly how Luka's mind worked. Both men were thinking ahead, something she had a great deal of trouble doing. She'd barely stepped out of the shadows of the past, to find a present. The future was a dark, ominous place where anything could happen. Seemingly, Kaine knew what he wanted and how to make it happen. Apparently, so did Luka. Kaine was right. She had to get up to speed. Things were moving exceedingly fast.

"What do you mean the end of the partnership? Luka works for you?"

It was then his words rumbled deep inside her like thunder.

He laughed sarcastically, but his face did not smile as he pointed out. "My Lady, if you'd done a background check, as you solicitors call it, you would have learned that Luka is as well known in the music industry as I am. In business circles better known. He has been my personal manager/producer for almost a decade. Without Luka, I would not be where I am today. The majority of people would say I work for him."

"Luka?"

This was news!

"Yes. Have you ever heard him take an order? I don't mean from me. I'm only fucking with him. Think back. No, I think not. It's one of life's cruel twists. Without him, you and I would have never met. It was his brilliant idea to put you in the Hard Rock video. Didn't he tell you the original cameo shot for the contest winner was a walk-on during a segment I wasn't in, or that the thoroughly revised shoot was Luka's last minute brainstorm? Apparently, he has accrued enough power at CMT to pull that off, and My Lady, that's power.

"Because of the quick change, I didn't have a script or storyboards to follow at the shoot. That was why he told me to enjoy myself. That bastard sat back and watched me fall in love with you and he captured it all on film, making sure I would be reminded when he took you away from me. That's power lady. Ironic, isn't it? He brought us together, and he will be the only one to destroy you, and I."

Holly was shocked by Kaine's words. He was right. Luka was in no way the man she had imagined — a simple, working-class man indeed! He was *the* man in charge, the puppet master. Too many pieces fell rapidly into place. Why he had left her that first night at the hotel, was to arrange to put her in the video. All the phone calls, he was frantic, yet powerful.

Her mind snapped, so acutely aware. She didn't want to think like a paranoid. But, again, was this all a setup? A Luka Hunter production? What sort of reprehensible man would do that? Certainly not her beautiful golden pirate with the angel eyes? But the evidence was stacking up against him. She didn't like the way she was thinking. What she said was. "Not true Kaine. Only you, and I, can let him destroy us."

Kaine shook his head in disagreement. "I know you're saying what you believe to be true. And it's your pure heart, and fighting spirit, I have come to love as much as the rest of you, My Lady. If your beliefs were about anyone else in the world, but Luka, your words would convince me. But think, you have already confessed he has revived you, making you feel alive. He has nurtured your transformation into a loving, sensual woman. You stated, you would have thought that feat impossible before meeting him. That is Luka's intuitive talent, to show people how to believe in themselves. I know, personally, that he has a brilliant imagination, sharp intuitions, and keen sensitivities because he can read people. However, his feet are planted in a solid reality he identifies with and moves about in comfortably. It was his brilliance that took me to the top of my profession."

"Your humility impresses me. You minimize your talents. Kaine, he's only a man. A man we can stop together."

"I'm not humble, just realistic. There are a lot of genius and talent, out there, but Luka was the chap with the vision for the band, and the only one with the skills to make it happen. You confessed you were falling in love with me, and still you wouldn't stop him from kissing you. You wouldn't stop him when he touched your body. No, I guess not. We can't stop Luka any more than I can stop the sun from shining. Believe me. He's only biding his time."

That was what Luka had said to her.

I won't be far away.

Holly slipped off the stool, moving closer to Kaine. She didn't like how she needed his strength, but he seemed calmer since his anxiety attack had evaporated. She swallowed, and looked down to him, fearing his words may come true.

Kaine lifted the bottle while inviting her to sit and join him. And what they didn't say to each other was perhaps as significant. If they could become a team to fight Luka, they could win. It was dark with the electricity out, and the central heat off left them to freeze.

The cold, musty air of the castle had numbed her to the bone. Holly lifted the bottle of orange juice and swallowed a giant slug. She choked, coughed, and then took another long drink. Kaine's cool hand pulled on her wrist to encourage her to sit on his lap. She accepted his invitation, needing his warmth about her, and thankfully melted into him.

Kaine sat quietly, wrapping his arms around her protectively. He held her, unlike any other time. There was no blazing passion. More a sacred warmth of love that enveloped her, different from anything she'd ever known, perhaps either of them had known. His heart pounded against his warm chest where her ear rested, reminding her, Kaine, was her future.

He relaxed his cheek on the top of her head. The scent of his broken breath was laced with oranges when he spoke.

"Luka has always been stronger than I am. He will take you from me. Surely, as the sun will shine tomorrow morning." He insisted with a beaten tone of voice.

Holly arched her back as the heat of anger rapidly coursed up her spine, setting all of her hair follicles on alert. She blasted Kaine.

"Are you going to hide? Let Luka take me? Well, I can tell

you. He won't have to take me. I will gladly run to him. I don't want a coward Kaine. I want a man." She choked back a sob.

"At least, Luka is willing to fight for me. Are you going to behave like the coward that owns Briarwood? And hide? Aren't I worth fighting for — isn't our love worth the fight? Please, you're my Precious One. Please, please, I can't fight Luka alone. I need your love to see me through … please."

"What do you mean to see you through, My Lady?"

"Kaine, my sweet love, think. I have to work with Luka for the next four days. He's the CMT representative. I have contest obligations to fulfill. Since we've agreed how influential he is, I will need your invincible love as a shield."

Kaine sat up, straightened his lean frame, and the movement of his muscles sent a wake-up call all over her body.

Her words seemed to revive him as well. Perhaps he would fight.

He moved her to stand.

She stood, and held onto the bottle as he gained his balance. The soft candlelight washed over him and made him look unbelievably handsome. The royal blue tapestry he'd had wrapped around him fell to the floor again, and her body stirred with a flash of enthusiasm.

With one great surge of strength, he picked her up, and he squeezed her into his body, kissing her, a lover's kiss, passionately telling her, he had made a decision.

Finally, Kaine had a plan.

Kaine pulled away and stared into her eyes. In a tone meant to squelch any doubts he proclaimed, "Of course, I will fight for you — for us. But if you leave me for Luka, you will speak my name and see my face when he touches you, it will be my kiss you remember. It will be me, watching whenever you're alone with him in the dark. It's my body you'll miss because he will never make love to you as I can. He hasn't the heart. Remember My Lady, from now on, the three of us are tied together like an Unholy Trinity, and you and I need all the help we can get."

Kaine's acceptance of the impossible situation scared Holly. She tightly wrapped her arms around his shoulders and placed her head in the warm nook of his sleek neck. As he started up the stairs, she heard the hum of the generators begin.

Kaine's strength impressed her as he wandered the castle, and up to the central staircase. Kaine stopped at the second landing and walked to the first doorway. She peeked in, and it was small by comparison to the guest apartment one flight above them.

This room was a bedchamber.

Holly didn't care where she slept as long as it was next to Kaine. She rested her worn and weary body against him, so glad she had told him everything — the truth so painful, and cathartic. She was more deeply in love with Kaine than she would have ever believed possible. There were no longer any lines of misunderstandings drawn between them. They had been replaced with truth and trust. The boundaries vanished. They were one in spirit and soul — soon to be one in the flesh.

She pushed any other thoughts of their future out of her mind. She had this precious time with him as she pressed her ear against his lusty male chest and counted the beats of his heart.

Holly placed the mouth of the bottle of orange juice to Kaine's lips. He slugged down another long drink. She took her turn swallowing the golden liquid. She looked into his soft, blue eyes.

Kaine returned to the fantasy dialog befitting the castle and vowed, "My Lady ... I will slay all the dragons for you. Tomorrow, I will fight for you, I swear until I have nothing or left for dead. But tonight I will make love to you, and I hope the sun does not shine."

His words, always surprising.

"... My precious love," she whispered in a peaceful tone.

He remained quiet, but his eyes were fighting, glowing, she had unlocked his warrior spirit.

She took a deep breath. Her sense of smell was undulating with the heavy, sweet aroma of roses. Kaine put her down kissing her all the while. Then they shared a drink and allowed the sweet juice to wash away any lingering trace of their harsh words.

She followed the sweet, perfumed scent of the roses further into the bedchamber.

He stopped her again. His lips pressed hers moist with the taste of oranges. His lips were full and insistent as he covered her mouth and sucked her breath away.

The heat spell consumed them as if a blazing fire. She felt his thoughts.

It was time.

Kaine turned by the doorway bent and grabbed the black satchel. He clasped his hand over hers, and then led her deeper into the pungent aroma of roses.

"Where is that amazing scent coming from, My Lord?" Holly asked as her eyes adjusted to the dim light of a candle he'd lit. The bed drew her nearer, and the beautiful bed cover was a braided gold color. It sparkled splendidly with old, regal threads that looked like if they were touched would turn to dust. The room appeared furnished with an armoire, desk, and chair of polished dark mahogany. Old World wood assembled to last for centuries as her love for Kaine. All the paneled walls were dark, topped with relief crown molding that had a subdued reflection from the glossy wax. On the bedside table sat a glass hurricane lamp on a swatch of bronze-colored antique lace.

"Kaine, what is that on the bed?" she asked, straining, to see in the dim light.

Kaine walked over to the bed table and lit the antique lamp filled with saffron-colored oil. From the glow of the burning wick, Holly quickly caught sight of Kaine's eyes. She read his pleasure as he enjoyed his surprise for her.

"I arranged this earlier for you," he explained, standing naked in the shadows of the lamplight.

She hurried to the bed and picked up a handful of the soft, velvet, red petals, then tossed them like confetti high into the air. They floated all about her crowning her head while she cried out with joy.

"Rose petals, Kaine ... the bed is covered with rose petals."

Kaine stepped in from the outer edge of the shadows clothed only in his love and passion for her. He dropped a few shiny square foils onto the centuries old night table. His hooded eyes were filled with love. His nimble fingers quickly freed her from the confines of the black velvet robe.

He stepped over the red rose petals scattered about on the floor. Kaine threw back the bed covers inviting her to join him in his love. He lay down on his back, pulling her with him and then explained.

"For now, you understand everything you need to know. But what is important is ... no matter what happens, you will never ... ever, leave me...."

His dreamy eyes made her stomach flutter while her heart pounded, and her mouth went dry, as she quickly agreed.

He rolled, swiftly arranging her body beneath him, molding his strong male body to the length of hers, and stretched out like a sleek, streamlined animal. He protected himself and then pressed between her legs a breath away from entering.

Her hands ran freely over his skin, up his arms, along his neck, to trace the lines of his face. His body was, so soft, and smooth.

He asked for no permission as his lips devoured her. Kaine invited her down into his deepest love, faster and faster.

Holly lost all sense of herself. When she could take no more, his hand stroked the warm skin of her belly, and down to where his finger entered her to make way for his hard fervor. He pulled it out, and she took all of him with one great thrust.

She welcomed him, wet, and hot for him.

Kaine pulled away and entered her again with another hungering thrust, filling her, firing her, loving her, moving into her, and out of her.

Kaine was determined to convince Holly that he alone could command the sun, not to shine.

Chapter Twenty-Two

MIRACLES

Day 4

It was a miracle. A fucking miracle. A clear sign of Kaine's invincible love for Holly. The dawn arrived on time, but the sky remained dark and ominous. Strange, thick, black clouds smothered the castle forbidding the sun to shine. There wasn't even a tiny stream of sunlight to frame Kaine's sleeping face.

Holly lay quietly in his arms, believing him to be an alchemist. How had he warned the sun? Banished it, sending it away? How had he alerted the Sun it would not be needed today because his love for her was everlasting?

Holly moved oh, so slowly, so as, not to awaken Kaine. She lit the last of the wick in the hurricane lamp, and it cast a soft, dim light. She looked at her magician and drank in every inch of his glorious face, his crescent-shaped eyebrows, and his long sweeping lashes. The additional growth of dark hair along his jawline, joined his long sideburns for one purpose, to serve and accentuate his radiant beauty.

He stirred. Kaine opened his sleepy lids and revealed his dreamy, dark blue eyes. In a gruff morning tone, he pulled her into him.

"Brilliant! Dreams do come true. I spent last night with the most beautiful lady in the entire world, and she is my lady," he exclaimed in a satisfied voice. He squeezed her tighter and added in a raspy, sexy voice. "You feel incredible."

Holly threw her long hair over her shoulder, dropping it down her back.

"I love you too, so much ... and, look, Kaine ... you have won! The sun does not shine!" She praised in awe of him, powerless to contain her happiness. She leaned down and kissed him long and sweet. She was in no hurry to break the enchantment. She wrapped her body all about him.

Kaine reached behind and protected himself. A moment later, he slipped the hardness of his sweet love inside her, melting her to him. Kaine stayed with her, celebrating for a long, long time. He reminded her of a thousand ways his love was especially for her, setting her spirit free to drift helplessly, rhythmically, in his exploding passion.

After Kaine had taken her to the depth of her pleasure, Holly lay limp and wasted in his arms. Her body flattened into every mold and crease of his. She listened to his heartbeat, and then as a fresh breeze, came the change.

Kaine twisted in her arms, to break the loving mood.

"As you can see I have regained my strength. And you, My Lovely Lady, should get going quickly, or I'll take you again, and again."

"Oh, you will? Then do it."

He threw her a defiant look as if to ask if she was challenging him.

She waited.

He called her bluff and protected himself. He faced her flashing those Technicolor blue eyes that declared he'd love her until she couldn't move, and then promised, "I'm here to please."

They started again.

Later, much later, when Kaine had taught her how to enjoy more pleasure than she'd ever known possible, she lay spent.

Kaine looked at her steeped in love.

This time, she knew there would be no more love. She crawled from the bed and tried to stand. Holly laughed and smiled graciously, looking down at him, knowing he never wanted to leave the nest. She stood barely out of his reach, and then crossed the room. Midway she laughed harder.

"What, so funny?" he asked.

"I can hardly walk. I hadn't realized I would be … so sore."

"Well, if I have anything to do with it, you will get much worse before you get better," he dared, joy steeped in his voice.

Holly hoped this was another promise he would keep. "Is that, so?" she bantered back, deep in love.

"Remember My Lady. You're with a man that can stop the sun. With you by my side, it's obvious I can do anything. Stay with me lady, you're in the best possible hands, believe me."

"Oh, I do believe, My Lord," she agreed, thinking over the hours of pleasure his hands had brought to her.

After a quick, soapy shower together in an adjacent

bathroom, she was delighted that they'd made love again.

Later, Kaine brought out a fresh change of clothes for them. They put on the clean Levi's, black *Hurrikaine* T-shirts that read *Lost Dreams ... Lost Illusions* across their chests, and then stopped in the kitchen to gobble a hand full of vitamins. They filled two beautiful golden chalices with strong amber colored tea and climbed the winding stairway to one of the two towers.

Kaine looked at the skies and was clearly as mystified by the weather as she. Kaine's facial expression grew more perplexed. They stood quietly searching the dark vistas of Briarwood Estate. The view, cloaked in supernatural darkness, accentuated a thick, ominous mist.

Holly leaned against him. The warm glow of her love failed to keep her warm on a cold English morning.

Kaine slipped his arms around her and held her tightly.

She decided this was the time to ask him. "Have you been married?"

Kaine took a sudden deep breath.

She hoped she hadn't wandered into dangerous waters.

He shook his head. "No, never found anyone I wanted to have a family with until now."

He was doing it again.

She pressed on with her next question. "Is that the only reason you would marry?"

"I haven't for any of the other usual reasons, again — until you. I've lived with women. Don't go thinking there was a swinging door," and he laughed one of his boisterous, joyous laughs.

Holly pictured his darling dimples, burrowing into his

cheeks.

"There were only three I thought I could build a future."

"Three? What happened?"

Kaine laughed again and then claimed, "Three isn't that much in my line of work. You sound, so serious." He hugged her tighter to put her at ease and then kissed her ear.

She accepted his answer. Three wasn't so many, considering his wealth and fame.

"There was a young, eager girl when I first came to England. We lived together, but she wanted my social standing and to smother me." Then his voice drifted. "Then another came along when the band was getting together. She was never truly in love with me, more the situation. The third one lasted a while."

She felt him swallow hard. This one must have hurt him.

"She came along when I first started making money. She was pretty, smart, sophisticated, what an up and coming musician needed. She eventually left me because I was too difficult to handle."

Holly looked up to Kaine.

He had quieted and was looking out over the dark estate. He sighed and spoke as he shook his head.

"The only thing I'm good at is music. The business end of music is rubbish. Until this tour, Luka has always been there to take care of me and seen to it that I received the best of everything. Music's been my life, rather taking the place of a wife."

Holly leaned on him thinking, Luka may have been right. Kaine did love the music more. Then Luka's words rang clear in her mind.

He will never marry.

But Kaine already said the words, even if he'd been playing a silly part to enhance the enchanting mood. And one thing for sure, with all his teasing, if he ever asked her again, the answer would be a definitive yes.

"You said you liked children? I saw you yesterday with someone's toddler, and when he was holding onto your shirt tail, you seemed, happy."

"Oh, Tristian, he's Chris, the bass player's son. I think it's great how Chris makes the music and family work. He takes his family on the tour with him. It's rough, he says, but not as rough as going home to find his kids have grown up without him. Tristan is a great kid. I'd like a few."

"Yeah?" She grinned. He wouldn't marry would he? What would Luka know about this side of Kaine?

"I would prefer a couple," he reiterated. "As a young child, I was raised alone too, and I always envied my friends with siblings. They seemed, happy, and never lonely."

Holly squirmed in his embrace and looked up at him.

He seemed sad, and Kaine sat down, his chalice of tea in an opening on the crenelated wall. He ran one hand through his hair. He took another moment and then his eyes became wistful and distant because the mysterious thoughts captured him again.

Then he spoke. "It was Mom and me. We lived in a tiny trailer behind a friend's cafe. It was hard for her alone, raising me. She waitressed days and sang at night in country-western bars as they were called then."

"Your mother was a singer?"

"Mom had a beautiful voice, best I've ever heard. We'd sit

for hours writing songs. She taught me to play guitar, so we'd play and sing together. They were the best moments of my childhood," he admitted growing quiet, and moody. He seemed to be cherishing his memories with his mother.

The sky changed a bit. The clouds gorged with rain, were becoming a lighter shade of gray, and threatened to become black and drown friend or foe at any moment.

Kaine took a deep breath calling her back to him, his voice smooth as a tonic.

"Mom was a lot like you. It was a unique and special experience for me to play guitar with you the other night. I've never shared my music with any woman, only Mom. It took me back to many happy memories before...."

Kaine's face tightened. Then his eyes narrowed. He was finished sharing. He looked down at her. His mood changed, his face hardened, and his jaw clenched. His blue eyes were dark and moody. Then, unexpectedly, he came alive, twisting her body into an unnatural position, kissing her as if she alone could banish the pain that ate away at him. His hands roamed her body, threatening to tear the shirt and pants from her flesh and make love to her there on the cold, stone tower floor.

Holly broke the kiss and grabbed a breath saying.

"I wouldn't get too carried away, My Lord."

"Why? Why would I want to stop and not make love to you, here and now?"

"Because you left the satchel downstairs," she pointed out smiling coyly.

He pulled her into his arms showing her his intense arousal as he slid his leg between her thighs. She shivered as his body lured her to him.

Kaine dropped another bombshell.

"Well, since I know your history, what are your thought about you and me starting a family?"

His words buckled her knees, almost knocking her down to the polished stone floor. She closed her mouth and stared into his calm, dreamy eyes.

"A what?" she stammered.

"You won't marry me, and you're my official girlfriend. I thought if I showed you what a regular chap I truly am, perhaps I could persuade you to raise a family with me. All you need to do is say yes." He recommended and then took a deep, short breath and raised his eyebrows that arched over sad eyes.

"I'm sorry, My Lady. You're not ready. I can see I am rushing you. I guess there's no more of my kisses for you." He smiled mischievously, his dark mood quickly lifting. He added laughter to his voice. However, it wasn't a satisfied laugh, more of a nervous laugh. He looked down at her, seriously looked at her, and confessed.

"My Lady, I see you, and I know what I want. This situation may seem to you that it's happening too fast, though, I've known for a long time what I want. I'm thirty-two years old, and I'm ready for love and commitment. I want marriage, and to raise a family with the right woman. And as the song goes, now that I've found you, I'm waiting for you."

What was she supposed to do with that? There was a proposal only it was one to have babies with him.

He looked up to the dark sky, and the mysterious thoughts returned. She wondered what his dreamy blue eyes were thinking about as his words clung to her heart.

Let's start a family.

I'm waiting for you.

Kaine paused, looked down at her with one of those beautiful dreamer looks, and with a breathy tone asked, "Don't you know yet? Believe it, my sweet, Lady Love ... my love for you is as boundless as the sky ... I'll never leave you."

The moment hung in her heart. The words seeped, healing, and a lone tear escaped to accent the heavy moment.

Kaine revived her, slapped her playfully on her Levi-clad behind, charging at her, chasing Holly as she squealed running down the winding tower stairwell. Her laughter filled the spiral brick cylinder as she continued the game down to the ground floor.

He chased her around the Grand Hall.

She turned in the doorway, heading into the massive state-of-the-art kitchen. Holly headed toward the butcher-block island, strategically set centered in the middle of the gigantic room. She darted different ways as he tried to checkmate her every move. He cornered her, running from side-to-side.

Kaine laughed and laughed, filling the enormous room with his wondrous joy. Then tiring of the game Holly stopped and let Kaine capture her, becoming a willing prisoner of love.

He took her into his arms, and her body molded to him perfectly.

Holly asked, "Is Kaine your stage name, or given?"

"Given. The official bio release reads that I arrived in the middle of a terrible storm, and while the quiet passed over, I arrived. One of the men at the birth said the weather reminded him of the hurricanes in Florida, and it stuck — Kaine, born in the eye of the storm."

"Florida? An Englishman was thinking of Florida when you were born?"

Kaine laughed and peered down at her. A gentle smile crept over his face and shaking his head as if he still couldn't believe he was a stranger to her. The words hung on the ends of his lips.

"I forget. You, my dear lady, are one of the few that doesn't know my decadent history inside and out. I'm so used to having my life watched, noted, and then quoted back to me with more lies attached until I barely recognize me. It never crossed my mind that I would meet someone who didn't know all about me. It's ... different. A pleasure for me to tell you about myself, for a change, the way it indeed happened."

He pulled her closer and sat down on a nearby ladder-back chair. He arranged her comfortably, straddling his lap.

"Okay. Kaine Walker, statistic number one. I was born thirty-two years ago in the good old U.S. of A., in Apache Junction, Arizona, near the Superstition Mountains, behind a small roadside cafe."

"You're ... American?" Holly was astonished. She tried to swallow a nervous laugh because of her surprise.

"You sound amazed? You don't like Americans?" His voice filled with a thicker British accent, quickly reminding her of Luka. This certainly wasn't the time to think of Luka, he was a train out-of-control, and she couldn't deal with him at the moment.

"Your accent?"

"Oh, that? I guess I've picked up the local flavor, possibly because I've lived here so long. Nope, I'm a red-blooded American boy. I'm a bit surprised too that you didn't notice last night, or how about this morning?" He cocked his head and winked. His face filled with his warm, sexy smile, but a hint of insecurity flashed in his eyes.

Good!

She probed. "What other secrets haven't you told me because you think it's public knowledge leaving me at a complete disadvantage?"

"Well, My Lady Love. A man in my line of work has many, many secrets. I'm sure I could keep your criminally trained mind busy for a long time unearthing my numerous scandalous adventures. I'll caution you. You will discover stories about me you won't like to hear. Countless things I'm not proud of, so please promise, you will come to me, ask me, and seek my explanations. Too many ugly things are believed about me that aren't true."

"Like your jealous temper?"

"Luka! Bastard! He's already started. Damn him!" He roared.

Holly was silent. She wrapped her arms around his shoulders and tightly squeezed him. She was a bit unnerved by his defensive reaction, but it wasn't all about Luka, she'd experienced his jealousy up-close and personal. She leaned back and looked into his storming blue eyes.

"I have been accused of many things," he complained loudly.

"But my reaction now is not acting like an ass or about being jealous of Luka. It's a gut-wrenching dread of the world separating you from me."

Holly leaned, and kissed him as a rock skipping over water. She needed to convince him, he wouldn't lose her. She stopped to nibble and then pulled his chin down to her in time to see his tongue glide across his bottom lip, inviting her, tempting her, promising to set her body afire.

Trust was a two-way street, and he was starting to trust her. Kaine Walker was at worst an outlaw, at best her hero.

She smiled while she kissed him somewhere in between his polarizing personas.

He must have sensed her change in mood.

"What?" he spoke between kisses.

Instead of telling Kaine, she changed her mind.

"Do you have any nicknames?"

She watched him drift back into time.

"When I was a boy, my mother read the stories about King Arthur and the Knights of the Round Table. After that, she'd called me Lance, sometimes, when I was particularly charming or made her laugh." He reminisced with a touch of humility while his face filled with peace.

Holly watched the increasing pleasure the memory brought to him, and she asked, "May I call you Lance, sometimes?"

Kaine fell silent.

Perhaps she had crossed over into a private dream, or memory she couldn't touch, or become part of, judging by his frozen reaction.

"No one's ever asked. I'd like that." He admitted and relaxed.

His sweet reaction delighted her, and she watched Kaine digesting her request, his eyes full of questions. She spontaneously blurted out.

"I love you, Lance."

"Say that again." He quickly urged.

"I love you."

"I hope you always do, My Lady Love. It sounds so incredible, feels even better." Kaine's sweet tone of voice punctuated his romantic expression.

Could it be? Kaine was as surprised as she that they'd fallen so quickly into this dizzy, spinning world of love?

Holly struck upon a great idea. She looked around the kitchen and scooted off his lap. She found a long-handled spatula and commanded him.

"Down on your knees kind, sir."

Kaine obeyed, and his hair fluttered in the air as he knelt. It finally settled on his shoulders, looking like a dark, royal cloak with the flat end of the spatula. She touched his shoulders lightly, first one, then the other, and proclaimed for all to hear.

"For giving me life, love, and laughter, I bestow upon you the honorable title, of my — Knight-in-Shining-Armor — Sir Lancelot de *Hurrikaine*."

His face filled with a generous, warm smile that shot deep into her heart. She could make him happy, and that was all that mattered.

"Then that officially makes you Lady Holly, the Fair Maiden."

They burst out laughing together. Holly was happier at that moment than all of the hundreds of moments with him because right then his eyes screamed how much he was in love with her.

"You, My Lady Love, see me," Kaine attested deliriously happy, filled with joy. He wrapped her lovingly in his arms, hoisted her up, and twirled her about as the tips of her toes scraped against the floor.

Tears brought a pinkish hue to his eyes again, and he gushed.

"After all, this time, I've found you."

Kaine set her down but refused to break the trance. Holly curtsied to Kaine and placed her hand on his.

He bent on cue and marked a trail of kisses to her neck. There he tucked his lips away in the crook of her neck. He pressed his moist, hot, lips as if he would perish if he did not kiss her immediately. And his kisses sent rushes of bumps sprouting all over her body.

With sweet, poetic words, Kaine spoke in a whisper. "I am your Lancelot. Believe in this new love of ours. Because what I feel for you means I will never, ever leave you — I promise."

Kaine's confession stole her breath away.

Woozy, she lost her balance.

He swooped in and kissed her again, and again, and again.

She hoped he would never let her go, but too soon, Kaine weaned her of his kisses, so — so sweet kisses and looked away.

A cold tone laced his voice. "We have to leave Briarwood. Time to face the world, I'm expected."

His rock 'n' roll wife had returned to demand him. But he'd kept his word. He'd given her his all, the one night in the castle. Considering the numerous surprises he'd created for her, she had no reasonable idea of what to expect next.

She took a deep breath vowing to take this miracle one moment at a time. She realized that to leave the castle brought a flood of bittersweet emotions. She wondered if they could keep this firestorm of love growing without burning out.

She had a plan...

Holly stood by the massive entrance.

Kaine picked up his *Hurrikaine* letterman's jacket. He helped her on with it and then continued to embrace her. He held her in his arms while the light scent of his cologne floating as a scented cloud from his jacket luring her to his lips.

"I want you to keep this Holly. Something to remind us of all the happiness we have shared these past few days. I want only happy things to happen to us. Then again, it's only fair that I warn you. I live a demanding, and exhausting existence. Things come swiftly, and the rules are different.

"Only special people can survive this lifestyle. I believe you're that special woman for me, Holly. I've seen it destroy otherwise competent people. I'm hoping, your love for me will grow strong enough to get through the fucked times. I warn you, there will be many.

"Always remember this. I promise to love only you, to take care and provide for you. I promise to slay all the dragons for you, My Lady Love."

As if to seal a sacred oath, Kaine kissed Holly quickly and hugged her for a long, long time.

He was a one-of-a-kind man on the run from his reputation as Kaine Walker — infamous rock star.

TO BE CONTINUED...

Dear Reader,

Please take a moment and leave a few comments about your favorite scenes wherever you purchased **PROMISES.** It is crucial to the series to have immediate feedback while the pleasure from the story is fresh in your mind. Thank you for your valuable support.

YOU ROCK!

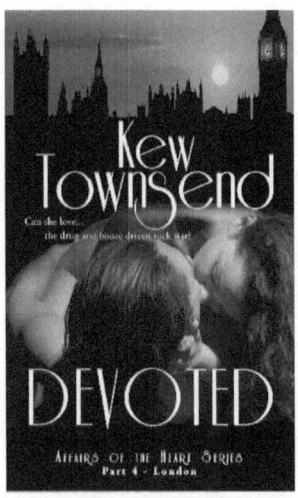

A happy woman...
Holly Hill didn't expect backstage rock concerts, celebrity parties, the paparazzi, or dangerous groupies when she fell in love with a rock star.

A gallant man...
Luka Hunter, a rock music executive, is the self-appointed protector of Holly from the dangers of a fast-lane lifestyle with a womanizing rock star. But who will protect her from him?

A magnificent man...
Kaine Walker, lead singer for the rock band Hurrikaine, has whisked Holly away to his decadent, fast pace, rock star world.

Can she love the booze and drug-driven rock star?

Find out in DEVOTION (Part 4) London

http://www.kewtownsend.com/

KEW TOWNSEND

Affairs of the Heart Series ~ London

HEART (Part 1), **TEMPTATION** (Part 2)
PROMISES (Part 3)

Forthcoming:
DEVOTED (Part 4), **BETRAYAL** (Part 5)

Ms. Townsend is a widow with a wonderful daughter, an educator, travel and movie buff, and writes romantic music fiction set in the 1960s-1980s rock scene in the *Affairs of the Heart Series*. She lives in sunny Southern California and loves to read under a palm tree with wave's crashing along the shoreline.

KEW's love of rock music began at a young age when she returned glass Coke bottles for change to buy 45 rpm records. Her interested moved from the music to the musicians, and living in Hollywood, interviewed the Beatles when they landed at Los Angeles International Airport. Acquiring a taste for the funny Englishmen, she began dating one of the Rolling Stones that exposed her to sex, drugs, and rock and roll. Later her memories surfaced in the *Affairs of the Heart Series* where she weaves her behind the scenes anecdotes with her long love of castles, mysteries, lightning, and thunder into a romantic suspense story. Her master's degree in Cultural Anthropology and Archaeology adds to her world travels, and flavor to her novels.

CONTACT KEW

kewtownsend.com

Leave a message, a review, and sign up for the NEWSLETTER. Be first to hear about new releases, preorders, sales, prizes, giveaways, and fun events.